THE FRENCH REVOLUTION

NCEBA TYOBEKA

THE French REVOLUTION

ISBN 978-1-77636-618-7

Published by Nceba Tyobeka using Reach Publishers' services,
P O Box 1384, Wandsbeck, South Africa, 3631

Edited by Gerard Peter for Reach Publishers
Cover designed by Reach Publishers
Website: www.reachpublishers.org
E-mail: reach@reachpublishers.org

NCEBA TYOBEKA
tyobekanceba@gmail.com

CHAPTER
One

Eliot was sitting in a dark corner of his low-cost house in Alexandra. He was thinking about how his great-grandparents had been ruthlessly murdered during the French Revolution. At forty-two, he wanted to approach the French government just to get clarity about what happened back then. *Perhaps I could get real answers,* he thought as he frowned. He was bewildered, angry and bitter all at the same time. He longed to know where his great-grandparents were buried. He yearned to find out if they were given a dignified burial or if they were merely tossed into the ground.

He was deep in thought, wondering if the families of the deceased were adequately compensated back then. He surmised that no care was for them during the

French Revolution, especially for the dead victims' relatives. He felt that, during those times, the French empire was greedy and cruel. After all, it was the 1870s. Did the royal family care about the rights of the people and gave those who died dignified funerals? He had read up about the topic in his history books but at the moment, he was not concerned about that. Neither was he concerned about who the king and queen were during the French Revolution.

Right now, all he was interested in was finding out what happened to those who died during that time. But, why now? Before dropping out of university, he studied history, one of his favourite subjects. He couldn't understand why he had an affinity for the subject. He seemed to have been badly affected by the Soweto uprisings and the Sharpeville massacres. So why did he love history the most? He wondered how his great-grandparents were treated by their own government during the French Revolution because from what he had learnt from the history books, it was a hell of a government. But if the French government was as bad as it was understood to be during the 17th century, what about the current government? Was it as terrible as that of Russia before the Second World War, during Stalin's five-year plan and Vladimir Lenin's reign in 1917?

Maybe the Russians could have been better then, or perhaps they were worse than anyone else, he thought. He was still sitting in the same position. He glanced sideways and then turned to look through the open window. He really didn't want to know what Stalin and Lenin had done. What he really wanted for now was simple and he seemed desperate to find the answer. He couldn't wait to see the French government in person and have a word with all those in charge. That's all.

By now, he should have completed his bachelor's degree, but his obsession with the effects of the revolution was the cause of his distraction. But why this after all the efforts he made? And why were his great-grandparents murdered and by whom? He thought and swallowed hard. Were the assassins arrested or did they manage to escape? Did law enforcement make a follow-up in connection with the case? Those were some of the questions he would have asked those in charge, but he wondered if he would be listened to in France because he was from another country.

He wished that the history writers were still alive so that they could help him find the answers., What he did know was that he would get what he really wanted. No matter what. After some time of sitting in the same position in the dark corner, he stood up. He turned and swayed like the mighty sea across the kitchen. He stood at the door but he didn't open it. Something was eating him, more than the deaths of the poor victims. *Damnit! Why were they murdered for God's sake? Who did this anyway?* he thought. He put his hand on the door handle but still, he couldn't open it. He then turned around and looked across the kitchen and to the photographs of his great-grandparents on the wall. He was mad at himself.

What was wrong? Was he sick? He thought quickly, and realised the timing and the way he was feeling was not right, Not now of course. He wondered how old his great-grandparents would have been if they were still living. He wanted to blame the French Revolution, its government and predecessor, the assassins and so on. He seemed to have hated whatever government ruled during the French Revolution. *At least, let them show me their grave and I will be satisfied,* he thought. His mind was racing so he decided to go outside for some fresh air. As he took in the morning air, the sun warmed his back. He was correct to want to go to France now. He realised that it would give him the sanctuary he needed and maybe if possible, he could find a chance to repair his ruined world. He leaned backwards, stretched out his arm and placed his hand on a tree trunk. It was dry and dusty. He knew his decision to go to France was the right one.

On the day of his journey to the merciless France, he still felt everything would be better and be over very soon. After that, he would return to South Africa. His thoughts were so encouraging. It was raining heavily but he continued. He didn't bother to share his dark umbrella with anyone, or his grief. Then the hail fell and beat against his umbrella. Still, he felt nothing; he was numbed by his loss. He wanted to believe that he could have done something to prevent his parents from being murdered.

He wanted to believe that they could have died natural deaths, passing away peacefully. That they should have died a natural death right next to him. And then he would mourn later when he could stand the pain. The bitter pain.

He could see his transport approaching. He decided to stop thinking about all the pain and hurt that was in him. He wanted to believe that his great-grandparents would have survived the killing if he had been there. He was comforted by the fact that soon, this would all be over and he would return to South Africa. He wondered why his great-grandparents weren't born here in South Africa but in France. He wanted to hate France and everything about the country. But why not hate the French Revolution and not the country itself? Why not hate the previous king of France and not anyone innocent there? Why not hate King Louis XVI and not his successor?

He was confident that he would find the answers he was looking for when he got to France. As he jumped into the white taxi, he was determined that he would not give up on finding out the truth. He was also looking forward to meeting the current king or the French government.

Although he was happy to leave for another country, he felt like his great-grandparents weren't given the attention they deserved by either the government or anyone else there. Not even the bloody king or his wife. Or even the useless French ministers and the state premiers. He felt like he should have been there during the awful days before they were murdered. It might have been exactly the same time when they needed him to manage things or protect them. He helplessly still felt as though his great parents were totally ignored by the honourable people he had trusted the most.

But why hate the king and the queen for God's sake? Why hate the actual French government which might have been so innocent at the time of the bloody French Revolution? Why not hate the current South African government? Why not hate the corrupt government of your own country? Damnit! How dare you? How can he stupidly hate the people who were not even there during the French Revolution? Why should he do that when the South African people didn't even have a hand in that tragedy? he thought bluntly. He wanted to cry but he just couldn't. Not now. Maybe it wasn't the right time. Maybe if he went outside he could weep freely. The thing that he feared most was that the girls would laugh at him, more than anyone else in the taxi. But why should he bother about the girls? After all, maybe they would show sympathy for him. He wondered if the boys would make fun of him if he cried. Perhaps others would say, "Hey *voetsek*." You know how men can be some-times. But not all of them were that stupid. Looking out-side through the closed window, he suddenly sat there motionless, without sensation or comprehension. But why care now? Why care for someone he hadn't even seen in his whole life? Why care more for someone who had died than for his wife, Fefe? Earlier today he had fought with her over this journey. She didn't want him to go. She was concerned that something would happen to him along the way. What if they met a lion standing in the middle of the road? What if....? What if...? There were so many what ifs.

It had been a long journey and the taxi was approaching O.R Tambo Airport. He was looking forward to the journey to France. Still, he couldn't shake that bad sensation; he couldn't even read a book or listen to classical music. Why not...? Why didn't he cancel the fucking journey and maybe do something other than this? Why not go back home and teach the village children about the very French Revolution he learnt when he was in school? Why didn't he? Why should he go to France when he knew that his great-grandparents had died a long time ago? What would he do there? What would he gain?

He was deep in thought, also thinking about his wife who was probably in tears at that moment. Why not go back home to the village and teach Lenin's war and the concept of communism to those needy farm children? Or Stalin's five-year plan to the different farms? Why waste his time and knowledge for nothing? Those village children would gain something from his great efforts. And at least they had their great parents beside them, unlike him.

The main thing about him was that he had never ever seen his biological great-grandparents. He felt it would have been better if they had died in his presence. He would have been satisfied and happy at the same time. He wanted to tell his story to one of the passengers but couldn't. He had wanted to blame the French government for his great parents' brutal deaths. He wished he hadn't been told about their demise by one of the people who had grown up with his great-grandparents in France.

Martinez, a retired medical doctor who had worked in several public hospitals, was the one who had opened up about the tragedy of Eliot Maphasa's great parents. He even added that they had a herd of cattle and more before they were murdered. Therefore, Maphasa was forced to get justice from the French government. Not war. He really didn't want to bring about hostility, especially in another country. But over and above, he felt like that government had been the centre and the symbol of his great parents' ruined lives.

Why did they arrest the perpetrators? The government had ignored and betrayed its own people. But unfortunately, they were gone now. Why didn't he just let them rest in peace? Why couldn't he let go once and for all? The government whom his great-grandparents had worked for on his behalf had left them to die. He felt like he had sold them out to the vultures of the world. The French government's love for his great-grandparents and everyone else there was now gone. But then he realised that it was too late and that the habit of loving them had long since replaced love itself. Those were his feelings, all the while thinking that the government didn't love them and he could never forget that.

What did you really expect from the kings of France with despotic powers and who only thought about themselves and their families? What do you expect from the royal families who were only concerned about their extravagance and luxurious lifestyles? The cab was still on the wet road. It turned left at a wide junction and this is when the passengers saw a strange red vehicle behind them. The passengers wanted to panic but were not sure of what the men's intentions were.

Maphasa was not paying attention to what was going on. He was trying to forget about his great-grandparents but he couldn't. He was not interested in the car behind them, the government's ignorance, his people or the panic experienced by his fellow passengers. He was deep in thought and swallowed hard once again. Suddenly, his chin hit the window but he didn't feel the pain. If he went out of the cab he would have smoked a cigarette. He would have stood apart and alone just to collect his thoughts. He also wanted to forget that the government had been the cause of his great-grandparents' lives' destruction.

Why couldn't he let go of his past? Why couldn't he believe that it would all be over soon and that he could move on with his own life? This time, he fell asleep because of overthinking. The person who had told Maphasa this story had died 25 years ago. He was certain that the doctor could have told him more. He lowered his chin and exhaled deeply.

"The French Revolution was unjust," he whispered. He didn't want anyone to hear what he was saying. All the while, the pain continued eating him inwardly, bit by bit. So why not share the story of the French Revolution with someone in there? Yes, share it with anyone at all. But still, it was not easy. Then, he remembered that he shouldn't have gone away because his wife Fefe Mandela didn't like it. He should paid more attention to her. He wondered what would happen to her now that he was away. The car behind was approaching closer. It was clear that its occupants had evil intentions.

"Hey, stop the taxi please," one of the car passengers said to the taxi driver. He panicked. Should he stop? Were his passengers in danger? Other passengers told him to increase his speed and he did so. He knew their lives were in danger. Now, Eliot started to recall what his wife had told him earlier that day but it was of no use to him now.

He fell asleep for a moment. He turned to the window so the morning son could warm his face when he woke up.

The car behind them was approaching swiftly and one of the occupants fired a gun into the air. The sound of gunfire awoke him immediately. His peaceful day was now devastated. Maybe in his sleep, he should have come up with more ideas as to how he should approach the French government when he arrived. Now, it seems his plan has been thwarted.

Damnit! What do these guys want from us? he thought as he looked out the window. His hands were trembling and he thought about beating them hard to break the window and escape but he couldn't. He shouldn't. Suddenly, as the red car had moved past the taxi, two of its occupants pointed guns at the taxi driver.

"Stop the fucking car, you fool, I demand it," one of them screamed as his aim remained fixed on the driver. Eliot should have jumped out of the window but he feared for his life and that he knew he would be shot by the thugs. He still wondered what they wanted from them. *Is it money or the taxi? What is it?* he wondered once again. All the other passengers in the taxi were screaming as gunfire rang in their ears.

The thugs did not intend to harm anyone, hence they fired shots in the air. Still, this completely frightened the passengers and they thought they were going to die. Both vehicles were travelling at high speed. Then, the front tyre of the taxi burst. The driver tried to control the taxi and brought it to a stop on a sidewalk a few minutes later. When the taxi stopped, the thugs opened the taxi's sliding door. "Guys, we don't have the whole day. We only need two guys. I'm afraid that the ABSA bank is lonely and is waiting for us, right now," one of them said.

The passengers in the taxi began looking at one another and mostly responded that they couldn't do that and that they had to go to their homes and so on.

"You are wasting our time," he yelled. Another shot was fired up in the air and the passengers began to panic. The thugs didn't change their minds. As a result, Eliot was chosen along with a dark guy called Patrick, a postgraduate from the Rand Afrikaans University in Gauteng. He was about to start a job as a teacher in two days' time. This was no longer the case. After a few seconds, they were dragged out of the taxi and pushed into the thugs' car forcefully. Neither of them had any choice regarding this matter.

Somehow the taxi not as full as the previous time, was left behind in bitter pain and sorrow. It was as if it would demand to know what was really going on there. The rain had stopped and the empty road worried everyone there. Now that Eliot was taken away to commit a robbery, what would happen to his French Revolution mission? *Clearly, the research work is already doomed now,* he thought as the red car sped on the dark road. He wondered where they were going and whether they would still be alive the following day.

After the first robbery had been successful in Cape Town, the two guys were released and dropped off at their homes. The thugs were dangerous criminals and had been involved in robbery, drug trafficking and kidnapping for years but they had never killed anyone. Patrick and Eliot were told they would be required once again when the time came. They were warned not to report anything about the robbery to the police, or else...

Eliot was traumatised by the experience. He stayed inside his house and didn't even disclose anything to his wife, Fefe, who was suspicious about his recent behaviour. Eliot knew that if he told her, she would probably report the matter to the police and he would definitely be killed. At least, the criminals had given him some of the stolen money. Although he was worried about his visit to France, he felt that the money given to him was better than nothing. He didn't envisage being part of that robbery and now by virtue of being forcefully taken he was an accomplice.

Why do these guys want us to do the same thing again? Why should they rely on us to commit such crimes? he thought. He wanted to tell them about his mission to France and that he was determined to complete it. But would the guys listen to his story, for God's sake? Eliot couldn't eat and was in danger of dying from starvation. Then, one night as he was seated in front of the wood fire outside the house he saw the same red car stopping at the gate outside the yard. It was the same guys who forced him to commit the robbery. However, this time their visit seemed to be friendly and businesslike.

The three guys had just turned up at his place to check on him. Their main reason was to remind him that they could return at any time for the move. It was important to them that Eliot kept his promise as they didn't like to be taken for fools. After chatting for a while, they got into the car, made a U-turn and headed off in the direction from where they had come. What they were looking for was far beyond his might. He waited for a long time at the gate and then he went back to the fireplace.

The streets were extremely dark. He went to the kitchen to take out the brandy and then returned to the fireplace. He stood there for a second and took a big gulf of the brander. He felt calmer and walked back to the kitchen before making his way to the bedroom, not to sleep but to think He looked outside through the window and saw the still darkness in the air. The sky was the darkest he had ever seen it. He was only worried about two things: the three guys and his visit to France.

When was he going to travel to France? He also remembered being told that his great-grandparents were the king's servants. He wondered if they were actually his bloody slaves. He still wanted to let the thugs know about the French Revolution and its effects and his pending visit to France. On the other hand, he was afraid of telling them for he thought they might turn it into a joke. And he wouldn't appreciate that.

He wanted to go back to the fireplace and place more wood on the fire to keep himself warm, but couldn't. His wife had long gone to bed. She was muttering and licking her soft lips in her sleep. He was cold, so he decided to sit on the chair next to the bed. Why didn't he sleep next to his wife? This time he wasn't looking down at the floor, instead he gazed through the open window. He could see the rising moon in the sky above the village but there were hardly any stars. He continued to sit on the chair. Then, he felt a sharp headache. Was it from all the worry and frustration? Why was he thinking so much about the French Revolution and his trip to France? Why not go to bed? Why not focus on other important things? After a few minutes, he finally fell asleep.

CHAPTER
Two

Two months passed and his accomplices from the robbery came to see him again. He wondered what they wanted from him this time. *Haven't I already done enough for them? What do they want now?* he thought. He actually wanted to ask them those questions directly but knew he would get into trouble if he did.

This time they had a strange request. "This time we need people with albinism, right." That was not a question but a demand and the words from Simanga were still flowing through his mind when they were about to leave. Eliot's girlfriend was out when the guys came to see him. Simanga stood by the door while his friends, Lesley and Peter, waited outside patiently.

Peter, who was tall and dark, was holding the car keys and kept moving them from hand to hand. What they were looking for was really a tough ask for Eliot. Not now. Not any time. Why didn't he report this matter to the police? Then again, what if the police were friends with the violent gang? This made him think twice about reporting them. His wife was still out when he agreed to their strange request. What he knew was that he was between life and death.

Why didn't he at least run away and find another place to stay? *You can run but you can't hide forever*, he thought. Then, the guys left for their place. When they left he was standing outside with them. He wished he couldn't have refused but couldn't. He was feeling the cold without his dark overcoat and he should have made the wood fire like the previous time. But he felt it was too late that night and what worried him the most was that his wife was still out.

He started to have negative thoughts. His heart was doing strange things. Was he having a heart attack? He was worried about his wife. She usually was home before 10 pm every night. *Where is that stupid woman anyway? Did she leave me for another man? Why did I not think about this before I decided to go to France, before the robbery?* he thought. Was it all too late now?

The house was lonely when she wasn't there. Yet, it still felt empty when she was there – it was a different kind of emptiness. She had not yet returned home. Why? What was the meaning of all this? Or was it beyond what he was going through? He still thought that Fefe might be cheating on him. What he felt towards her (wherever she was) she felt towards him as well. What he had done wrong towards her she must have been doing it to him.

He sat on the black couch, his eyes were black. He looked through the dining room window as he tried to recall all of his mistakes. He was sitting there all alone when the gang turned up again. They wanted to know if he had found what they were looking for: young people with albinism. He wanted to ask them, "Don't you get tired of this thing?" But he couldn't do that for he knew that he would get hurt. He had already known what he was going to receive in turn for his insult. Such people were not the ones to be insulted; they were unkind and ruthless, regardless of their crocodile smiles. He had ter-rible feelings towards them and wondered if they were going to keep invading his privacy by showing up at his house whenever they wanted.

Why didn't they mind their own business? Hadn't he helped them enough already? Why must they keep coming to his house? He must have been coming down with a fever lately. He wasn't impressed that they had shown up once again. He was also worried about his wife who had still not returned home.

"Please, find the beautiful albino girls for us right?" one of them demanded. They laughed as they stood next to the cupboard in the kitchen as they waited for his response. He didn't respond to their question. Instead, he told them to come back in a few days. He knew he would be out of town then. Most times, the guys didn't sit when they visited him. He added that he wasn't feeling well and that they should rather call him first before visiting him. As the months passed, Eliot's scorn gave way to impatience and irritation, irritation to anger. What angered him the most was that the three men seemed to be too stupid to understand what he was going through or how he now felt about them and instead of visiting less frequently, they continued to appear more than ever before. Soon, they were coming to his house almost every day. Even though he chased them away, they just didn't budge and that angered him. This time, he left them waiting outside the gate for hours; they were not going to tell him what to do.

Another thing was that they completely ignored his instructions as to which days they should come. He would go inside the house and sit on the couch alone quietly. Eliot seemed to be as silent as the previous time but more persistent than required of him. The road outside was empty and quiet. He went outside again to see if they had returned but they hadn't. No. Not today. He looked up and down the length of the street and there was still no sign of them again. They were gone. But his ignorance and him leaving them waiting outside could be dangerous for him and they might retaliate. He had driven them away so why was he feeling guilty? Still, he was relieved that they didn't return that day.

He wished that they wouldn't come back again. Still, he wondered where his wife was. Had she left him for another guy or not? Was this a form of revenge because she had decided to leave her alone while he pursued the French Revolution? Was there any profit for the French Revolution in turn now that he nearly had gone there? Would Fefe also have the same thought as him that he was cheating on her and that he lied about going to France? When he was obsessed with this French Revolution they didn't make love as much as she would've anticipated and at most times she needed to be intimate with him. But he didn't care. In fact, he wasn't in the mood.

Was it because of his desire to get to France? On the other side, he wished the guys didn't return to his house. He didn't want to keep on ignoring them when they showed up because they were dangerous. Even though he benefitted financially from the robbery, he could still land in jail. The guys didn't know how much he hated their visits. The depression and obsession to find his own lover might have been the main reason. But why didn't he touch his wife at least before he almost left for France?

He fell ill with flu and lay feverish in bed for days. During those days the guys didn't come back and he liked that. *Thank God!* he thought as he exhaled deeply. Why was he so blind and stupid to ignore her? When last did he kiss her romantically? How did he pursue the French Revolution issue more than his relationship with her? His thoughts were reeling and he didn't want to feel devastated. That's how it was with him. He wished she could have been there in the bedroom, waiting for him to wake up in the morning and lay down with him at night. Surely, he was going to have enough time together with her at home but now she wasn't there. She still hadn't returned his calls or made any other contact with him ever since her disappearance.

He wanted to forget that he would probably never see her again. It felt as if she wouldn't come back and he wanted to give up on her but couldn't. She was still his soulmate, how could he possibly do that? He stood up from the couch as usual, walked across the floor and leaned backwards against the wall. He peeped through the window, looking into the distance. He thought he could see her coming back home. That would have set him free forever.

He needed total freedom and to be loved like the previous time. He felt like there was enough love from his wife, plenty of it. And freedom. He also had freedom. Freedom from his anger and guilt and obsession with that wife of his. But living together with her again would be living a lie, waking up beside her every morning, parroting, "I love you every day and night." The thing was that he didn't want to wait for her until he got tired.

When last did they hold hands or kiss each other? The main thing in his thoughts was whether he should go to the police and report her sudden disappearance. But it wasn't an easy task for he knew that he might be arrested for the robbery. Also, what if she was found murdered? What would happen to him? The police would certainly ask why he didn't report her missing. They would also ask how long she was missing for and if she had any enemies, etc.

His feelings made him want to go around and look for her. He had gone looking for her in town a while back but he couldn't find her. He wondered if she could really betray him or maybe she was being held hostage somewhere. Why couldn't he report the matter to the police? He swallowed hard that Monday morning and immediately realized that he wasn't feeling well. Why didn't he ask for help from the neighbours at least? His thoughts had almost made him look insane. Was this the result of his impending visit to France? Why didn't he listen to her from the first time? With the French Revolution, what he hated was Louis the Sixteenth who had treated his servants like trash.

According to Eliot who had a good knowledge of history, the French empire had never loved the clergymen and the Bourgeoisie. And everyone else. He wished he had never studied history, especially in Grade 10 where he learnt a lot about the French Revolution. Eliot had spent days suffering without his wife around him. But he

felt something big was coming or was going to happen
to him. He no longer thought about the guys or the kidnapping and robbery.

However, after one week of waiting for nothing, he
received the bad news that she was coming home pregnant and alone. That had made things harder for both of
them. She wanted to explain to him why and how it happened but not over the phone, of course. That night he
felt betrayed. It was also his birthday and he had hoped
he was going to enjoy it at home with his family. But, now
he had to deal with this. He didn't want to believe it. He
had never been so hurt ever before in his life. He wondered why she didn't take his calls when she was away
and where was she all along.

Although he was feeling betrayed, he still loved her with
all his heart. How many hours had he spent alone in the
dining room thinking about this? He sighed deeply as he
lowered himself on the chair and turned around to look
away. He was now seated uncomfortably. He was thinking about how all this had happened. Had she been
cheating on him all along? He still wondered why she
didn't take his calls when she wasn't around with him. He
didn't have to remind her about going to Paris, hence
there would be a hindrance. He stood and turned right
to walk into the bedroom. He walked very slowly like a
somnambulist. He wanted to blame himself for all this
nonsense. The jealousy inside him had nearly killed him. It
actually felt like it was suffocating him.

He sat there on the edge of the bed as he looked out the window. He thought, looking straight at the window to the outside. This wouldn't have happened if he had decided to leave for France that night. He wanted to blame himself again for the same reason. He sat there on the edge of the bed thinking about who had impregnated his wife. Why? He thought that by sitting all alone in the dark bedroom he would find the answers but he didn't.

If God hadn't brought Fefe into his life... If things hadn't played out the way they did with her life... How were they going to deal with the fact that she was pregnant by another guy? He somehow felt like things between the two of them would never be the same again. Was it because of the pregnancy or was it because of the way things had been between themselves during her disappearance? He felt as though it was better to die than to go through this. However, at the moment, he wanted the truth from her. She really had no reason to keep the secret but she wasn't sure how to make him understand that she had messed up and was raped by Mandla from Tembisa.

Who said she must go there and for what? He wished she was here already so that they could talk and then move on with their own business. But how? How would he be happy when he was feeling devastated? Most of all, he wondered if he would manage to pretend that this wasn't his kid now that she was pregnant. He wondered how his siblings and aunts would feel about this:

the unknown pregnancy. They might even feel betrayed by both of them. And that was something he couldn't risk for he knew that he would feel weak and useless in the eyes of the public. But the public had to understand what had happened or they must find out all about it. Why? He took in a deep breath and exhaled slowly. He really didn't know what he would do about it. He looked at his thighs and felt the familiar stinging in the corners of his eyes.

Then, he looked into the distance at the mountains of the Puguma Forest. The temperature was dropping now and it was in the late Autumn that she would be back home. He was happy that he would see her face again, her smile but he ached at the same time. It felt like it was the biggest loss that someone unknown had impregnated Fefe. But if she had finally disclosed the fact that she was raped, how would it be easier for him to believe that? However, he felt there was still no room in his bleeding heart for someone else no matter what.

At last, he stood up again and walked back to the kitchen to make some coffee. He wasn't interested in sleeping that night. The heart, his bleeding heart, was the main reason for that. He stood there in the kitchen and looked at the kettle without doing anything Ever since his great parents had been murdered in France. he had never been okay. But why think about that now? Did he want to think about the French Revolution again and

King Louis XVI, his clergymen and the nobles? Finally, that Wednesday morning, his wife arrived back home.

He took a good look at her and realised she was still as beautiful as before. He just didn't know what to say to her. *Something like this has never happened in this relationship before*, he thought as he looked at her without saying anything. He really didn't know whether he should congratulate her that she had come back home or not. But the pregnancy... He realised that if he sent her away, she might do something worse than this. He felt still and unnatural.

Would he still be in love with her regardless of the pain in his heart? Would he still touch and kiss her romantically as they used to during those beautiful days they shared before? Can he trust her like before? But why can't he accept immediately that this had happened to the woman he loved? Why can't he accept immediately that what is done is done? Or why can't he just send her away if he wasn't really satisfied with her presence or the pregnancy itself? But the fact was that she had managed to tell him that she was raped by Mandla. However, it was a total lie that Fefe had told him because it's said that she and Mandla had been romantically involved before she dated Eliot. And during their relationship. She wasn't honest with him at all. The reason was that Eliot would probably be angry and then tell her to pack up all her belongings and move the hell away from his house, isn't it?

CHAPTER
Three

Meanwhile, Eliot was now broke and as a result, he was tempted to kidnap an albino girl by the name of Sophie from the Tsako village. When asked by his only trusted friend Peter Miyambo from Mozambique, he claimed that the president, Cyril Ramaphosa, hadn't yet deposited his three hundred and fifty bucks for four months. He was now tired of waiting for nothing. On the other hand, he remembered that he had to support Fefe financially and emotionally now that she was pregnant. And very soon she would have to give birth to her baby boy.

Eliot who was six feet tall and with a heavy build was a big dark man. However, everyone in Tsako village knew that he was not capable of unnecessary violence. Nor was he hostile to himself or anybody else in the world.

He originally came from Zimbabwe where he used to blame the late Robert Mugabe for the unnecessary violence used on the white farmers and the poverty he had caused to his citizens. But now that he had kidnapped someone's child, the beautiful young albino woman with blonde hair, can you still say he wasn't hostile to the public?

Sophie's mother, Kate Lwandle, was going through a lot. She was worried and in despair, frantically wanting to know where her daughter was. She desperately wanted her to be found and the police had made endless promises that they would find her. Sophie's mother could hardly sleep. She just sobbed helplessly and even claimed that the police weren't doing enough to find her. Sophie had been locked up with another guy, Thabo Mapetla, in a dark, rusty shack in the dark forest of the Vaal Dam River. When Thabo was out in town, Eliot would take over the job to look after her in that dirty, stinking shack.

Thabo, from Alex township, was in his early twenties and was supposed to have completed his bachelor of science at the University of Potchefstroom that year when he took up the job of kidnapping job young albino girls and stupidly decided to drop out of university. He had bluntly claimed that there was so much money from this kind of assignment than being at university for long. He had dark hair and skin and he was handsome as fuck. His good looks were part and parcel of his persona. All young and old women were attracted to him, no doubt about that. But all he really wanted for now was the damn money, not any women or anything else.

Sophie was placed on the missing list and the last time she was ever seen was at the Rand Gate Mall with an unknown guy who had offered to give her a lift home. The stranger was Thabo but no one knew who Sophie was with in the blue sports car. The number plate wasn't identified when it was checked out from the CCTV cameras. However, the police have been trying their best to find the young girl. But anyone e who might have thought that the police weren't desperate to find out the whereabouts of the girl, it was a lie.

But why hadn't she still not been found? Why wasn't there any clue about that? Through the heavy darkness, the girl opened her eyes and felt immediately threatened. It was after Thabo had gone out to town to do some shopping and party with his friends. It was pitch dark and she realised that she was bound, both hands and her beautiful feet tied. Never before had she experienced something like this. She was now living like a prisoner and didn't know what was going to happen to her. She didn't know that she was going to be sold to the highest bidder. According to Thabo, a deposit of R1 million has been paid into their account for her to be taken away for rituals or anything they would want to do with her.

She was just an innocent girl so why must she be sold out for Heaven's sake? she thought as she cried silently.

What she had realised was that most people with albinism were denied their rights to freedom and regarded as something to prey on. Most of her relatives and friends had been murdered and others sold into drug trafficking. "Why?" she asked herself. And besides, she never wanted him to realise that she had been weeping softly. But why abuse women and children, especially the innocent people who have never caused any harm to anyone in this world? What she knew on one level was that she was in serious trouble and wanted to accept that.

Sadly, her dad was no more. He had also been murdered as part of a ritual. Her worry was that she was vulnerable and could be raped by anyone in this bloody fucking shack, stinking of all kinds of shit. She wondered who might come in tonight to monitor her or even rape her. Who had been hired to carry out such violent activities? What had the South African government done to prevent all these kinds of violence and hostilities towards women and children? What had Thabo Mbeki done to stop this nonsense when he had been president of Mzansi? What had the late Nelson Mandela done to defend women and children from being victims of murder, rape and drugs? What role did Jacob Zuma play during his term in office as president of the country? Why can't South Africa be like other African states and protect women from all kinds of violence?

She had been thinking hard when she heard a vehicle stop outside. She started to panic. Who was coming out of the car now? The gloominess inside the shack was still dominant and there was no way that she could outrun or stop it. What she knew was that she would be victimised every step of the way tonight.

Tonight was tonight. She silently swore! She had been all alone almost the entire. This time it was Eliot who got out of the car. It was his turn to look after her and even make her feel loved. Make her feel free. But how would she ever feel free when her freedom was already denied by the ruthless predators of Tembisa? She had just remembered that she had to return to university the following week. But she couldn't because now she was being held hostage. She wondered how Steve Biko overcame the beatings and all the dangerous activities he had experienced in prison before he died. She wondered how all the Robben Island prisoners must have overcome the difficulties of their lives there before they were set free.

Can she ever overcome this kind of life of being locked up every day and night? What did she do to deserve to be in this situation? But now that Eliot had come back to monitor her, what was the future of the French Revolution? What about his pending visits to France for him to achieve his answers from the current French government? Was there any more hope that he could ever go there in order for him to get permanent freedom? He thought as he waited outside the shack and he knew about the situation inside it. But did he care anymore about that? Or did he only consider the money first and then the French visit afterwards?

He put his hand deeper into the trousers pocket and took out a packet of cigarettes. What he knew was that he got the money at last and the R350 rand grant was nothing anymore. However, he still wanted to go to France and nothing was going to stop him. Sophie strained her eyes to see where she was being held captive but the darkness was still dominant. When she thought of her future, her dying future, she cried openly this time.

Why must she hide that she was crying and she had the emotional pain of death inside her heart? She wanted to blame whoever had done this to her personally. While she went on crying helplessly, she wanted to put her hands on the shack wall but couldn't. There was nothing to see there at all, it was completely dark. She couldn't really understand all this, that she could end up being in here and being wrongfully punished for nothing. She had a home in Tsako village that was not only full of love for her but was extremely beautiful. She had everything she could have desired and a great opportunity to complete her tertiary education. A good life right ahead of her. Not this kind of jail. What was exactly the meaning of this anyway?

Meanwhile, Eliot was busy smoking outside and he hadn't been concerned about the way she was suffering inside the bloody shack. Did he know how much she wanted to go out of that place now? He tilted his head once and leaned backwards against the same shack while looking at the dark, dancing trees. His bosses had trusted him more than his other accomplices, including Thabo, who had started to party and get drunk every day.

This meant that Eliot had the opportunity to be trusted the most than him. Although this had worried Thabo, there was nothing he could do about it. He knew very well that he had blown it. And besides, his bosses, Abdul Rahman and Ike Chukwu from Nigeria, were already disappointed about his actions. He wasn't to be trusted any more. This gave Eliot more power and money than before. Although he had managed to support his wife financially he was losing interest in her. Maybe it was because he wasn't spending as much time as he did before she decided to go to France. He was starting to resent her.

The full moon seemed to travel from one spot to another and he looked at it. He wondered if he could be free like a start and go wherever he wanted. this was the true life right up in the sky. Whether he could live there alone or together with the astronauts and learn more about that kind of life and stuff. After a few minutes, he went into the shack. He didn't want to remember the way he had been a very poor man in this world. Besides, he didn't want to blame the South African government or the current president for his poor background.

He looked at this victim and became quiet. He just didn't know what to say. It was still dark inside and he couldn't even light a candle. He was instructed by his bosses that he was not allowed to do so as this could attract the attention of passers-by. The Vaal River forest had become more quiet and scary. But he was used to that, and besides, the guy had been waiting for the truck to come over and transfer the girl to somewhere where a cruel fate awaited her.

He looked away and then turned his head to shoot his gaze upon her. There was still nothing she could do now that she was being held hostage. He looked at her for the third time and still didn't say anything. Not that he wasn't interested in sharing a moment with this beautiful young woman. What he knew was that she was more gorgeous than anybody else. But he braced himself and became a gentleman. In turn, she was still scared and his silence made her even more frightened.

She had never felt this way before. She was used to her own house, not this one. And besides, he was a total stranger to her. She wasn't even used to Thabo who was now regretting losing his job. Eliot felt the urge to speak to her but he felt that he should get closer to her. As he moved closer, she swallowed down the scream that she could feel something building inside her throat.

He knew that she was scared from the very first time he had entered the shack. He looked at her face in the darkness and she was quiet too. She had never let anyone know that she was afraid of anything or about the way he was watching her right next to her. She again thought that he might consider setting her free. Why didn't he talk to her at least for God's sake? All her life she had been living very well and was always safe. She wasn't going to let this dangerous matter mess her up. But why can't he say something to her or do what he had intended to do to her?

"Are you okay?" he asked at last but didn't touch her. He seemed to be smiling at her.

She took a deep breath to calm herself down. She could hear her heart pounding like a drum. *Why not say something better than this?* she thought grimly. She was impressed by his slowness. It bothered her more than the thought of what was going to happen to her. The shack was eerily quiet. There was no sound other than her own breathing. What she knew was that it was not good at all. But it wasn't making sense. What bothered her the most was that she was never accustomed to waking up somewhere strange without having known how or when she had arrived there.

She stared at him in the same darkness and responded, "No, I need to go back home right now." The way she had answered him clearly indicated that she wasn't begging and that she was demanding. However, she tried to control herself and the anger inside her.

But why didn't he release her once and for all? He didn't want to think about going to France again for he knew that he would not concentrate on his job. But he seemed to be more impressed by her natural beauty more than anything else. What would he say in turn in case she said she had fallen in love with him? What about the job that he was given by the Nigerians?

Sophie looked at him again and didn't say anything. She didn't want to see any strange man sleeping beside her and had no idea who he was or where she had come across him. What she wanted him to do now was to untie her. Yes, she was tied up and she was in immense pain. From that moment, he never said anything more to her. Instead, he deliberately became quiet. It was not that he was not interested in her or angry. But the thing was, she was feeling the physical pain.

She also felt the fear rising inside her chest. He definitely wanted to let her know how beautiful she was in turn but wasn't feeling what she was going through, (he wasn't afraid of anything). But he didn't intend to rape her or do anything wrong to this young albino woman. All that mattered for now was for him to let her know how terrible he was feeling for her. It was really indicating that she could make a good wife of tomorrow.

If things could go right or the way he wanted it to be it meant that this young albino woman would not go anywhere. It also meant that she was going to be taken away for human trafficking or something. What she knew was that she was going to be killed either right there or taken somewhere else and killed during a ritual. She knew how her previous friends had been killed after their strange disappearance. She missed everyone at home. She missed almost the entire world. She missed her beautiful life, including her total freedom. She still had the same qualities she had had at twenty-one. Men wanted to reach out and touch her. And she liked that attention, whether she chose to let them or not. But, that wasn't a point.

Through the darkness, she wanted to stand up as tall and beautiful as she had been. Everything about her was beautifully done, carefully thought out and well-maintained. She had spent a lifetime becoming who she was and she would have done it well at university. It was too bad that she hadn't gone further in her career. She wondered about it sometimes but she wanted to give up now that she was locked up in here. She was the hottest item in town and many men wanted to be in a relation-ship with her.

However, she never felt it was too late. She wanted to pray for the first time and then closed her eyes. She wondered if she must do it inwardly or not. He kept on watching her and he realised that it was now 10:23 pm. He looked towards the door and then directly at her face. Just watching her always made him feel good. Why didn't he untie her for relief? A few minutes later he stood up and went out to get some fresh air. Why didn't he go out together with her? Obviously, he should have done so but he didn't want to risk his life by making his Nigerian bosses angry.

The first thing he had wanted was for him to be safe and the rest would follow. He didn't want to die or be killed for money. He smoked for more than thirty minutes outside and besides, he wanted to check out who might come into the shack or attack them. As quiet as this forest was, no one was to be trusted there. No one or else. He could always untie her but then he wouldn't be trusted any-more once this had been found out. The important thing for now was trust and safety. He knew how the Nigerians had been working with him or whoever it might have been. They would kill you if you didn't play your cards well. One needed to be careful with them.

The silence around her inside was complete like the dark-ness and no one would ever see her or hear her in case she started screaming. But then, she knew that there was no need for her to do so. Screaming unnecessarily would only make things worse and the guy wouldn't trust her. She had been held captive for some reason she didn't know and she just hoped that the reason would be explained to her sooner or later. But she wasn't interested in getting to know whatever reason; what she wanted now was for her to be released and return home.

Finish! she thought angrily. He was still outside when she tried to get up from the dirty mattress. Somehow, she was feeling cold and besides, one couldn't use that stinking black and white blanket. She wondered how many people had been kidnapped and held hostage in that shack and used the same blanket. How many victims were held hostage for different reasons? How many innocent young men and women had been abused by the Nigerians for their benefit? Did Eliot think about that now? Had he felt that pain before himself? Of being victimised, especially by strangers, for their own business? But what seemed to be irritating her the most was that she was supposed to have been far with her future and she had always known she wasn't here for any reason that might benefit her.

Why didn't he take off together with her and disappear forever? Why didn't he make her become his wife instead of a slave to someone who didn't have a heart for other people? He was still outside and she really needed to use the toilet. She felt a sudden urge to open her bowels and she was coming down fast and yet she could feel it. It was like that with all the victimised people when they were held hostage. In addition, she hadn't eaten for four days. She was worried about the situation she was in. She had never expected this to ever happen to her.

Out of her desperation, she tried to bring her hands out from behind her back but she couldn't. She shouldn't. They were tied together extremely tightly and as a result, every movement brought about a burning pain. She regretted going to the bloody mall where she was kidnapped by these thugs. She blamed herself for going to the mall alone instead of staying at home and watching television with her albino family. This time, she realised that even her remaining family at home wasn't safe; they could be kidnapped at any time. All she wanted to do now was beg this guy to release her.

Suddenly, she heard Eliot outside talking to someone over the phone. She couldn't tell who it was but then she began to worry that she was going to be taken away. She was concerned about her life. She wondered what was going to happen to her now that Eliot had been in touch with someone over the phone. She wondered if she was going to be raped. Had she not gone to the mall by herself, she could have been home right now, reading anything by Eskia Mphahlele or Ngugi Wathiongo.

Suddenly, she took a few shallow breaths and the panic lingered close to the surface. She closed her eyes tightly and tried to relax her body but it was hard. *No man, can you please release me? Set me free forever, please,* she thought faintly. This time, due to the bitter pain around her limbs she wanted to scream terribly, but she paused. She was still fully clothed and clearly, no one had tried to rape her or had attempted to do so.

A few minutes later Eliot came back inside. He closed the door. He didn't want anyone to know what was happening inside the shack. Once again, he was silent and this irritated him more than before. *Why? Why must I be treated this way as a young woman in my own country?* she thought silently.

The man kept on watching her from the door where he had been standing. What he knew was that he couldn't just allow her to leave because he knew how dangerous the Nigerians were and he feared for his life. He was a kind person but he knew he couldn't release her for now. The timing was bad at the moment. *Can't she just wait for some time, at least?* he thought. He swallowed hard and he wanted to let her know that he would release her and tell her that she would be safe but he couldn't.

When she began to look at the dark wall of the shack, she missed her home again. Of course, she really missed her mom the most. Tears formed in her eyes and she blinked them away. The main thing was that she was furious and the anger inside her was growing. Still, she wasn't ready to show her fear to him or whoever was sent out to find her. She had actually known very well that Thabo had kidnapped her. She seemed to hate him more than anyone else in this group. Yes, it was a serious kidnapping obviously.

The current feeling gave her a thrill of anticipation that maybe her mother would pay the ransom money. She was feeling vulnerable. Also, she longed to eat something and drink. She was weak and afraid that she would die from starvation and thirst. She mostly craved something to drink, Coke or Sprite soft drink. That would be fine with her. When last did she have some drinks or snacks?

Although it was dark there in the shack, her eyes held his for a long moment and she smiled blindly, completely forgetting that she was being held hostage. He was someone she would have liked to know better and he had never shown any signs of aggression towards her whatsoever. There was a quality that drove him wild, a sensuality mixed with a cool reserve that made one want to tear her clothes off just to see what the rest of her looked like. He really suspected that it looked damn cute. Cuter than he could imagine. But he wouldn't have minded if it didn't.

Though he smiled silently, the thought of her haunted him almost all night and he was no longer sure what he wanted from her. If he really wanted her for his sexual feelings or for himself or both. All he knew was that he couldn't stop thinking about his feelings for her. He watched over even though he drifted into sleep. He knew that he couldn't sleep on the job. Was she now tired? Would she sleep through the night on the stinking mattress?

Why didn't she invite him to join her just for fun? When she asked him to remove the rope from her hands and feet, he did exactly as requested. Immediately after that, she had fallen asleep. There was no time to talk to each other any longer. She was exhausted and slept like a baby on the mattress. She didn't even smell the stench coming from it. She snored softly and he smiled to himself when he heard that. But he couldn't compare her with anyone nor would he do that to his wife either. He was now beginning to wonder.

He didn't seem to give a damn about anything except her connection. He was tired too but he waited for the right time to sleep. He hated going home these days. Even his dog looked unhappy. And he felt so guilty. Had he found another love? Even after three weeks, he couldn't go back home. He wondered why. But the guilty feeling built up bit by bit inside him. He wondered what his darling was saying or if she wasn't concerned that he hadn't returned home.

He wondered if Fefe would blame the French Revolution and his visit to France again. Did she care anyway? Yet he seemed to be earning well from his illegal activities. But would it be fine if he betrayed his bosses by taking this woman away with him? The feelings inside mounted bit by bit for this woman. He wanted her more than he had wanted any other woman in the world before. Every time he looked at her he swallowed hard as if he could eat a thick steak. He craved her like hell. She had been weak for days and could eat less than he had anticipated. He had bought the food from various cafes, so why didn't she eat well? He had given a minimum amount of water but a lot of drinks like she had wanted.

She was always feeling thirsty but the hunger wasn't so acute any more. All she really wanted for now was more drinks and then to go home. Or should she take off with him to somewhere where they would never be found again? She hated being there or being taken away by the bosses.

She couldn't understand how she was brought to that place. She seemed to sleep more than necessary and she thought Eliot might have put something in the water and the drinks to keep her sedated. But she had no guarantee about that. At least he had untied her hands and feet but still manacled around her ankles. She hoped she would not be tied up again unless he didn't love her. But she was still in the bloody darkness with him all day and night. Sometimes there was light when he brought her water and food. He used a torch but it blinded her eyes.

She had a feeling that he was interested in her but he hadn't said that to her. She told him that she still missed her home with her entire heart. She missed her siblings. She could no longer hold back the tears and started to weep.

This morning, she had woken up earlier than usual because she heard the whining vehicles outside the shack. Eliot went to talk to the bosses. They wanted to know if he needed anything and if she was giving him any trouble. He said no and that she was fine. After some time, they left. Even though they had left, she started to panic wondering what was going to happen to her.

She thought that something was going to happen to her tonight; maybe she would be murdered. She just didn't know what she would do to survive the pending danger or what Eliot and his bosses wanted from her. She could smell her faeces, she could feel the dirtiness of her body and clothes. She hated the fact that she was drenched in sweat.

When he returned inside, she felt he would be weird towards her. He waited there in front of her and kept quiet. She waited for him to rape or assault her but he didn't do anything. What she wanted for now was justice or for him to run away with her. What she knew was that these Nigerians could return at any time and really hurt her. That thought terrified her. She felt that the man was very slowly acting against that. At least, he was being kind to her by bringing her food and water at regulars and he emptied the chamber at some point. He also left her some blankets. Still, she didn't know whether she would be alive tomorrow.

The transfer of the girl was now imminent and Eliot had been told that he should be ready to go to town and await final instructions. He seemed to be more than worried because he was falling in love with this young albino woman. On the other side, his wife, Fefe, had been angrier than she had been for a long time. She was still pregnant and even contemplated committing suicide because Eliot had not returned home. She was not going to tell anyone about her intention to kill herself. She had let him down so many times in the past together with her friends when she had disappeared.

She felt she wasn't going to get another chance to be happy with Eliot. *But why didn't she approach Mandla, the baby daddy for their own happiness and not with me?* he thought. He did want to give her the attention she needed but couldn't. The main distraction was the coming baby and he knew that and that it wasn't his. She felt like she had already lost her lover and besides, they weren't married. But she had lost him many times now. The pain of each loss became more acute, it never lessened. It was the pity she had hated the most. She knew that she could deliver the baby on her own but felt that he wasn't there for her anymore and that he might have found a new love.

Why didn't he answer her calls or come back home to her and the baby? No, why didn't she call her baby daddy or go back to him? Why keep bothering him and not her baby daddy? Her silence now meant no one was watching her every move, questioning every expression on her face and asking if she was feeling fine, or if she was of colour, telling her to sit down or lie down as if she was dying. The main problem with her in the house was the loneliness and fear. What if she was attacked by his friends who kept visiting her frequently after they could not find him in the dark forest?

She sat in the kitchen and after a minute, she dialled his number. But he didn't answer her call. If he was in, she would have sat there right next to him and smiled gently at him. The house now felt much bigger and she felt very alone without his presence. It seemed to scream loneliness and didn't feel cosy anymore. Still, it was the only home she had and leaving the house would be admitting that they would never be together again. *Why don't you come home my love,* she thought to herself. She didn't even realise that she was weeping.

CHAPTER
Four

Meanwhile, the Nigerians went to the dark forest and neither Eliot nor the girl was anywhere to be seen. Eliot was being paid well to watch over the girl, so why betray his bosses now? The main reason was the feelings he had for a woman he loved. The bosses couldn't trust him anymore. He had disrespected them. Why would he sacrifice his life for that of the girl? Just for his own feelings towards her? The bosses thought about his possible betrayal and were not happy with him.

They returned to the forest on Wednesday night and still, there was no sign of Eliot or the girl. Eliot was reluctant to lose his job and yet, he was running away with the girl. The Nigerians were drug dealers and their main priority was to find Eliot and the girl. They were wound tight with nerves and they were expecting him to show up. But he didn't at all. Tired of waiting for him, the bosses decided to send their two other trusted men from Limpopo, Ndakhulu Malo and Mhali Mokoena, the most dangerous hitmen ever, to go after Eliot.

The two men were the best assassins in the country and didn't waste any time when hired to do a job. However, this time they were instructed not to kill Eliot or whoever they might find along the way. They tried calling him but he wasn't answering his phone. It was 2 pm on Wednesday and he was nowhere to be found. The red light on the phone was flashing furiously but he ignored it. He really didn't want to deal with the calls at the moment. His priority was the albino girl's safety. He was feeling numb.

As the time passed, the two men began to get angry. They wondered what they should do to find him but didn't know where to start. *How dare he?* one of them thought as they drove around town in a red car. How dare he not rush back to his bosses, throw himself at their feet and apologise profusely and beg for forgiveness so that the matter could be over? *How easily he had lied,* one of his bosses thought in disgust as he put the phone down in their office.

They wanted to have control over the situation and to find him immediately. However, Eliot wasn't ready to bring back the girl. He knew that if he was found, they would kill him. He considered telling him a lie that the girl had been kidnapped by someone else while he was away but he knew that his bosses would find that hard to believe. Still, he wanted to protect the woman until he was certain that she was safe. He was somewhere in a village called Matlapeng where his childhood friends had matriculated. He knew that he wasn't going to give up because of his love for the albino woman.

His love for the albino woman had made him reach boiling point and he felt a cold sweat wash over him. "God!" he exclaimed. He had predicted that he would be in this situation today. All the dirty belongings had been left in the shack in the dark forest. He really didn't know what to do at the moment but he knew that he should stay put where he was. The young woman should have gone straight home but then she claimed that she didn't know who could be behind her back. She knew that someone was after her life.

Thabo Mapetla was reappointed in his job. He was given the task of finding the albino girl. Eliot begged his wife to come to the village. She finally relents and agrees to meet him and bring some of his stuff along. She was angry and jealous because of what he had done to her. Not to mention that she was pregnant. She looked at him with contempt and he felt humiliated. She told him the words that he didn't like to hear. She even insulted the young albino woman. How dare she do that to a stranger? Eliot managed to calm her down. Besides, he had wanted to know if the Nigerians had been looking for him. She said they were.

"They came by three times and after that, I never saw them again," Fefe said frantically. She was so angry that she wanted to beat him up. But she couldn't. He had always liked the way she looked at him. It made him feel good. Her jealousy was boiling inside her. Eliot's life was totally in ruins. The two hitmen had been looking for him all over town and elsewhere.

After some time, he glanced at the bathroom door resentfully. A sulking woman was the last thing he wanted. He could hear the running water. Couldn't Fefe understand how traumatic this was? He wanted to go into the bathroom, not to bath but to think. He knew that he would take a bath later. Inside, he was happy that he was with the two women. He thought that Fefe was being selfish and unsupportive. He was already in the bathroom when he looked outside through the window. He had been feeling guilty that he had betrayed his bosses for the first time.

Meanwhile, Fefe had indicated that she was worried that she might lose her baby to the hitmen if Eliot didn't show up. She kept imagining that she heard their vehicle outside her house and had sleepless nights. She didn't want to recall the scene she had with Eliot earlier today. But, she wondered if he still had feelings for her. Stop woman! How can he have feelings for him when there is a young albino woman next to him? The way he was looking at the albino woman, it was as if though Sophie was an egg that would crack.

His feelings were reserved for the albino woman and not for Fefe. He knew he couldn't tell her that for he knew she would be more furious than before. But he didn't know how devastated she was because of his love for the albino woman. Was she of so little consequence that hurting her didn't bother him? Was this the real Eliot she knew? The questions whirled around in her brain, torment-ing her, grieving her until she couldn't stand it. The tears welled up and rolled down her cheeks and she wanted to bury his face in his hands. But he wasn't going to feel guilty for the rest of his life. He didn't kill or fight anyone.

He was between two women now. That's Eliot. Yet Fefe had been expecting to be touched and to be loved by him. But a twinge of disappointment ran through her. He tried to pretend to love her like before. His actions of taking off with the girl made it clear that he no longer had a crush on her. She still wanted to find out in her heart if he really loved her. Even before he tried to travel to France. But the crushes came and went. Over a decade ago now. But Fefe didn't exactly understand why her boyfriend wasn't happy to see her. What she saw for now was the actual frustration in his face and fear. According to him, she should be on her own and go on with her life. Her heart will go on alone.

He glanced towards the door and smiled. What was it now? Did he see or hear something? He half expected her to walk away from him but instead, she headed towards him. She was still deeply in love with him, no matter what. But the pregnancy had been the main thing to him for he knew that it wasn't his child. Of course, he wasn't responsible for that, so why didn't she become honest with him? A deep yearning welled inside her. She wanted to be touched and he wasn't interested in that. He pretended that he wasn't feeling well and that he couldn't do anything romantically with her.

Calling him tonight into her bedroom would be useless. Saying she wanted to hear his voice was true but he didn't want to do that either. Other men might love a surprise love but not him, not this way or under the circumstances. He wasn't like the previous men she had dated before. But looking at him in the face, she wanted to talk to him and she wanted to remind him that she still loved him and even more than that.

The young albino woman remained alone in the dining room, watching television. She didn't complain about anything. He took a deep breath and exhaled slowly. The main problem with him was that he lied to Fefe that he still loved her. But there was nothing he could do with her at this point, not under this state. Besides, he seemed to have lost his feelings for her but couldn't tell her because he realised that his life could be in danger. What if she disclosed where he was hiding with Sophie to the Nigerians? He needed to play his game very well, otherwise he could die tragically. He was frustrated by the situation he had found himself in.

Why did he refuse to kiss her just for the night? She looked at him in the face again, hoping for a sign that he had had a change of heart but she saw nothing. Absolutely nothing to suggest he felt or wanted her more than the previous times. Fefe thought that he had feelings for that bloody girl. She wanted to know if he dated this poor young woman with albinism and he said no. When asked why she was here if there was nothing between them he responded that he needed to protect her. He actually denied that they were dating or that they both had feelings for each other. It was his own secret. Besides, he didn't want to rush things or spoil this relationship. Fefe told Eliot that she still had feelings for him and he just nodded and kissed her just to push her away.

What he knew was that he would sleep right next to the albino woman. He was adamant that he was going to do so but an irritation burned inside Fefe. She forgot about telling him how she felt about him. But then she wanted to tell him about the pending future between the two of them. But she wasn't going to give him the satisfaction of knowing how much she cared about him when he didn't or wouldn't admit how he felt about her. Annoyed at the situation and at him, she raised her chin. However, her goodnight kiss suggested that she was still into him. What she knew was that she wouldn't let him go. She wouldn't give up on him. Otherwise...

At that moment Eliot might still like her or even care for her. But he would downplay whatever he felt because it would be hard for him to deal with it. Distancing himself rather than admitting how he felt would be much easier. He liked to be famous. He liked her very much. But this... What she really wanted from him would be too difficult for him to deal with. On the other hand, he also felt betrayed that she had been impregnated by someone he had never known. Why didn't he say it openly to her so that they would get a way out? He had thought about it.

Why didn't he tell her the truth and what he felt about the pregnancy? If he couldn't be honest with himself, how could he ever be honest with her? Bottom line, he couldn't. Even though her heart was splintering into pieces, she needed to understand that she was wrong. That her demand of him was a bad idea. She couldn't force him to love her again, especially after the bitter disappointment she had caused.

After sitting alone in the dining room, the albino woman eventually went to bed without letting anyone know.

"Do you love her?" Fefe demanded to know and Eliot smiled blindly. That was easy to answer but he wasn't expecting her to ask him that question. She searched his eyes needing to know the truth and willing to believe him. She trusted him just as his Nigerian bosses did before he betrayed them. There was something about him that seemed scary and she sensed correctly that he would still betray her one day.

She remembered how he held her hands the night before he left for France and took her in his arms. That was the last time he had ever shown her any real love. The head-ache was too much for her; her anger, her terror over the albino woman and her sheer exhaustion. A few questions came to her mind. What if the hired hitmen had returned and were now looking for her? What if they have killed her next-door neighbours? Yes, she was worried about that and more than that. She was desperate.

She watched him walk slowly into the bedroom where the albino woman was sleeping. She wondered if she should follow him. She sat on the edge of the bed and closed her eyes. It was very dusk and there were a few stars in the sky that she could see through the bright cur-tains. As she sat there alone, he wondered if he would still love her in future. She wondered if she could still love someone again. She had sensed something was wrong and she didn't want to go back home. She felt as though the house had been haunted and that she would be haunted by it if she had returned there.

If he really loved Fefe then why humiliate her, lie to her, cheat on her? Why bother to be with the albino woman if he wasn't in love with her? Had it been a lie from the beginning? But remembering their sweet, early days, she couldn't believe that.

Ten days later she went away back home. She had given birth to a beautiful baby boy named Lucky. She was fully aware that Eliot continued to support her financially but not emotionally. At least, he still tried his best as a man. Eliot desperately yearned for the good old days with Fefe but the pregnancy betrayed him. After two months the guys have arrived again at the house. At the time, Fefe was in the house with her aunt Meme from Mafikeng.

"Where is the guy, Eliot?" one of them asked, holding a gun in his hand. Both men stood at the door as if they were expecting a sudden attack upon them.

"I don't know," she responded adamantly. She had been holding her baby, clutching him to her warm chest. *What is going to happen next?* she thought nervously. They looked around and like the previous time they were gone. They had no intentions of wasting time. They were obsessed with finding Eliot and the woman with albinism. They still didn't know where to find him but they were determined to do so. So much so that they hadn't slept; they were sweating more than anything to get him. They agreed that when he was found they would torture him. After all, when it comes to drug trafficking and kidnapping, mercy is an unknown word.

Two months later, the hitmen came back to Eliot's home one night. This time they were more ruthless. The instruction from the bosses was that they should murder him if it was found out that he had anything to do with the albino woman's disappearance. Fefe and her aunt were busy cooking in the kitchen when there was a knock at the door. Who could it be at this late hour? When Fefe's aunt saw the two of them again, she almost fell to the floor. Fefe went to the door and when she saw them, her heart was pounding furiously. Something inside her told her that there was going to be trouble.

What do they want this time? Fefe thought to herself. She really didn't expect them to pay a visit tonight but the men's deadly intention was adamant and she knew it. Eliot was the person they wanted. That's all.

"Where is the guy?" one of them asked as they both stood at the door. It was after Fefe's aunt had opened the door for them but they didn't want to go inside. But this time they felt like they had been fooled by her and their facial expressions showed how angry they were. Mercy is an unknown thing even today. Anything could happen right now. Suddenly, the tallest of them stormed into the house holding a gun in his hand. He opened the bedroom door and looked around but there was no sign of Eliot.

He returned to the kitchen in silence. It was evident that he was infuriated. There was a quietness that prevailed over the entire village. Pedestrians and motorists were scarce at that time of night. The silence seemed to indicate that there was a calm before the storm. "But you know very well…," Fefe answered with confidence. She was tired of their frequent visits to her house, especially when she knew that Eliot wasn't around. "Now that he is not here, why do you still come here all the time?" she asked. The two guys didn't seem to believe her. "But you know him. You know his exact whereabouts, don't you?" one of them said. It was impossible to speak to him anymore. He was a large man and was throwing his weight around. Fefe had been about to make some coffee in the kitchen but couldn't. The fear gripped her.

Fefe's aunt stood there, her eyes downcast and said nothing. The man took in her appearance. She was extremely attractive and a little bit thicker than they had anticipated.

"But you know him. You know where the man is right?" His words indicated that they were both inhumane and unkind. Besides, they could have paid someone else to find him but they were determined to find Eliot themselves.

She looked at him for the third time and noticed a mixture of shyness and aggression. Even more than that, she felt like shutting the door on them as he was speaking. Somehow they didn't seem to speak too much because they knew that there would always be an alternative way to find Eliot.

"I don't know where he is, okay? Where must we take him from? Do you see him here because when he left he didn't say where he was going to," Fefe said in a half whisper at last. It was the way she said it made him look at her more closely.

Although she had whispered, her tone hadn't been servile or pleading. She spoke as if she would ask for a speedy apology and then regret it afterwards. She spoke in a manner that was not herself that was not quite a demand, more of taking something for granted. You see, they wanted to go away but there was something they didn't understand about her. About both of them. How can they live here with the baby alone without the presence of the father? The absent father! They had seen her face and eyes clearly but sensed they were mocking and laughing at them.

"You know his whereabouts," he repeated and he knew that he sounded foolish and stupid. Then suddenly, she maintained her silence, refusing to look at either of them. She was afraid that she would say something that she shouldn't say and needed to be careful in choosing her words. Finally, the two hitmen walked away.

She knew they would return but their leaving was a sign of defeat. But why should they be defeated as men? There was no answer or was there? All she knew was that they would return. She wished that Eliot had been here with them. Was he going to protect them if he had been here? But maybe she thought he could deal with them physically. But he wasn't going to stand their guns, isn't it?

At last, after making coffee they went back to the living room to talk. What she knew was that they had to get away from them. Even though the guys had left, she was still afraid. When her aunt had gone to bed she resolutely went outside to see if anyone was lurking around. But there was no one there. No one. The quietness was even more evident now. The night was gloomy and there was not even a star in the sky. Even now as she waited outside under the green trees there was a long, long silence. Her head was bent and she had a look of visible pain. Being left alone in that house was traumatic for her.

There had been many long nights when she and her aunt had been unhappy and lonely. What could have happened to her and her baby if her aunt had not been there for her? Maybe she might have been murdered along with the baby. All she knew was that some men never had a heart. That they can just kill. On the other hand, she wanted to sell all of Eliot's belongings because he was not answering her phone calls again. He didn't even bother to call to see if they were okay. She wanted to make him feel hurt more than she had intended. She would take some of Elliott's belongings to her uncle's house in Benoni. For the first time in months, she began to feel the same confusion and headache she used to feel at the hospital before she gave birth. That was the same strange pain somewhere in her head that made it impossible to think or decide on anything.

All she could think of was this bloody man Eliot. She wondered what he was doing with that woman with albinism. She wondered what made her so special compared to her. Sometimes, he felt lonely without her for days but there was nothing he could do about it. She also felt lonely without him. She had tried to call him on numerous occasions but he didn't answer. Now, she was getting ready for the move to Alex together with her baby and her aunt. But can she overcome the way she missed him and how he used to kiss and touch her in the early days of their relationship? Before the issues of the French Revolution with him?

CHAPTER
Five

A few days later Eliot was over the moon. That was after the albino woman, Sophie, had agreed to fly with him to France. He still wanted to go there and complete his unfinished business with the French government. He was more determined to achieve this, with or without the woman. He should have done that long before he had decided to come here into the village. On the other side, although Fefe was about to leave for another place, she still missed him terribly. But that was another story. A story he tried not to let himself think of any more.

The memory of her was very painful. Those unforgettable eyes, her lips and the bottomless sorrow she wore like a wound the last time he saw her. But then he hadn't seen her for seven months. Seven months without seeing her, touching her, holding her or even knowing where she was and telling himself it no longer mattered. But it did matter to him anyway.

However, Fefe together with her aunt were on the verge of going away to another place. They needed a new permanent space where they would be at peace. They couldn't live there anymore without a man, and that was Eliot. He was really needed there to be their pillar of strength and to help them get through this difficult situation. Fefe didn't know that the two hitmen had rocked up at her house again.

The red car had approached the house silently. The women were carrying bags in their hands when they knocked on the door. They soon realised that the women were about to leave. The bags they were holding were a clear indication that they were not coming back to the house. Why hadn't they told the men before that they were leaving for good? In that way, they would have stopped coming there. Looking at what they were doing, the hitmen surmised that the two women were concealing something.

"So you decided to leave behind our backs? Huh?" one of them said rudely and the reality of who they were was revealed automatically. The brutal anger and the ruthlessness in their facial expressions were clear to see. It felt like the end of the world. Who knew what was going to happen to them? What had those hitmen planned to do with them?

This time the guys were not in a rush and came inside the house. They asked Fefe to make them tea. She tried to resist but she was forced to do so. The intention here was to cause unnecessary delays. She looked at the short guy and turned round to drop the bag to the floor. She had never felt betrayed and devastated like this before. Her aunt had the baby on her back.

Fefe seemed to face the actual predicament they were in and had hoped they would be gone by the time she returned to the kitchen. They didn't seem to move and eventually, being tired of waiting at the door, they decided to sit at the table. She decided to have a cup of coffee while playing for a time. The coffee was served at gunpoint, and after some time the conversation started. This visit was pretty much like the previous one.

It was a dark and gloomy night when the hitmen turned up again. This time the short guy was determined to speak first. He usually didn't say much on the previous occasions that they visited. When Fefe's aunt asked what her name was, she mumbled something like Thuli. But the surname was audible. But the guys didn't bother to ask her to repeat it. Somehow she seemed afraid of her own voice. The truth was she wasn't accustomed to either of them, and was a little afraid. When asked where

Eliot was, the women said they didn't know. Then the two men were forced to take off with the baby boy.

"No, you can't do that," the women protested but they had no choice. The baby was snatched from them at gunpoint. They were devastated but they knew that going to the police would be of no help. What if the hitmen were waiting to see what they were going to do after they took the baby?

Fefe thought a lot about the situation. They had to come up with a plan to get the baby back that didn't involve the police. Fefe wondered if she could trust the guys with her baby or if they would kill the child. How could she give up her own flesh and blood to these hitmen just for Eliot's sake who didn't care about her anymore? Also, if Eliot was found, how would he fulfil his assignment to France? Her aunt was frantic and just stood in the kitchen as the hitmen made off with the baby.

After a while, Fefe walked to the door and peered through the long corridor. It was loadshedding so the entire area was dark. She stood by the door and then realised that she had to call Eliot. She knew he wouldn't come home so she slammed the door and went back to the dining room. Her aunt had already gone to bed. She walked around the house wondering what to do. Finally, she went to the bedroom and slumped on a chair beside the bed. She wanted to read her book *Othello*, but she suddenly lost interest.

For God's sake, why must they come to her house? What had she done to them? What had she done for them? She felt guilty that the baby had been taken away with the guys and had sacrificed the child to save Eliot. She had told them lies and she knew it. Why couldn't she just tell them the truth? She thought grimly and immediately stood up to lean on the wall next to the window. She was feeling guilty. If had told them the truth she would still have her baby and the hitmen would not return to her house again. On the other hand, if Eliot had been found and murdered, he wouldn't have completed his French Revolution assignment. Fefe would never see him again.

Who would warmly kiss her again like him when he is dead? She thought selfishly. What was the meaning of all this? Why was she more concerned about Eliot's safety than her baby's life? Why didn't she report the matter to the police? Fefe tried to contact Eliot that entire time but he wasn't available on the phone.

She eventually went to the village where he and the woman were hiding but they were nowhere to be found. Perhaps, Eliot knew that she would return to the village and would lead the hitmen to him. It was clear that Eliot and the woman had disappeared and he never bothered to tell anyone about his whereabouts. He didn't trust anyone with his life. He had known that life comes once and a single mistake would end it all. He didn't want Fefe to know that he and the woman had checked into the Roodepoort Hotel for their protection.

Meanwhile, Fefe and her aunt had been at large when the two hitmen had come back again to Eliot's home. But Fefe was nowhere to be found. There were no signs of her or her aunt. Unlike before, the house was not locked. So, the two guys stepped inside and sat on wooden stools. One of them was holding the baby.

He was feeling guilty about taking the child from his mother. He knew that the baby missed its mom. He wanted to tell Fefe that he was sorry for what he had done. The baby wept tearfully sometimes, but the two hitmen didn't bother much to return him, afraid that they might get caught by the police. He really wanted to tell Fefe how he really felt but she was no longer around. He felt something rise inside and choke him. He had never felt this way before. He felt like the mother of the baby had died, but she was alive somewhere around Alex.

Why didn't they find out more from the neighbourhood? The other guy was as silent as if nothing had happened, he had looked sideways. They left with the baby and didn't return to Eliot's house for a few days. They were worried and didn't know what to do. The short guy wanted to find her, hug her and tell her that they were sorry for taking her baby away. They had done the most foolish thing ever. Why didn't she go to the police and report the bitter crime, especially about the kidnapped baby?

A few days later, they went back to the house but Fefe was not there. Fefe seemed to be the main target and not the aunt. As they waited outside the house they looked into a cheerless pall of smoke. They felt deserted forever. Would she ever return?

Is this all just a dream? one of them wondered. He thought that maybe he would see her in town one day. Both men just stood outside the house like statues without saying anything. They were feeling guilty. This was the first time they were tasked with kidnapping a child. He again thought that he would meet her one day in town. If it happened, he would tell her everything about their wicked past and the reason they were committing those heinous crimes.

He knew that he had been forced into a life of crime because the government couldn't provide for its citizens. But why didn't she call them because she had their contact details? What was she so afraid of? They didn't have her contact details so she was the only one who could initiate contact. How foolish she had been!

Fefe was still in Alex. One day, she thought about how she was willing to contact Eliot but not the hitmen to find out if her baby was still alive or not. How distant she sounded! How useless she had been! Her fury intensified and she seemed to be blaming herself for all this. Maybe, if she had contacted the hitmen, she would have been reunited with her child. She regretted her careless mistakes. Why was she still so desperate for Eliot to love her? Still, she believed that while she was hiding in Alex, she would come up with a plan and have a better understanding of the situation.

She believed that her baby would be returned. She would sit down there behind the house in the garden, listening to the singing birds and feeling the fresh air. She felt as though there would be no need for her to keep loitering around but to find the baby or report the matter to the police. She felt there was something in the Alex garden, the tender human adjusting herself to herself in the soothing impersonal presence of the cool trees and grass and earth, before going out into the stare of the world.

However, it was so strange and it was the first time since she had experienced this bitter pain. Yes! That was the first time and now she sat there every day and read a lot. She read her book *Othello* but she was distracted at times. She had actually wanted to be alone in that Alex township garden. But how would that help her get her baby back? On the other hand, she didn't stop calling her boyfriend Eliot.

Why didn't she call Mandla? And the police? And where was Mandla while she was in Alex? Then she felt as though there was no happiness. She felt like she had no life there, she felt it go slowly. Ever since she had come to Alex. Ever since she lost her baby like that. But she felt it was ridiculous.

After a few minutes, she went back to her book. She would never go anywhere without it. She had read it even when she was in Grade 12 at Manqoba High School. But she used to love history. She felt it pressing up, coming, coming, dark crushing, ready to burst but then she knew that she would always turn away, just in time back to her book. That was her system, of course. That was the only way she was going to do it. She would let it come near, irresistibly near, time and again, ready to catch her alone in the same cool garden.

Why didn't she invite her aunt to the garden? This was becoming a serious habit now. She didn't read all the time though. She would regularly put the book down and look around, watching the birds while they sang in the trees. But one day she would find the baby, her main friend in this world. Of course, one day she would find that she had achieved what she had always wanted. She would feel as though she had always been like that. She would feel the eternal happiness of this universe. But would she ever get her lover back as she also needed to overcome this cruel loneliness? For now, her main concern was whether her baby was still alive or not. She didn't care much about Mandla. She felt as though he had been a big distraction in her life. The biggest hindrance.

CHAPTER
Six

After some time, the shorter of the two hitmen showed up at Eliot's house. He had decided to return the baby to his mother. Fortunately, the baby had been in good shape and he definitely looked healthy. But he must have missed his mother. He probably had forgotten about his mother. When last had he been breastfed as a two-year-old?

The red car had waited outside the yard. The concerned guy held up the baby in his bold hands with tender care. He went to lean against the window and peered inside the house. He knocked on the door later when he realized that no one had been coming to his help. *If only I could find his own mother*, the hitman thought bitterly.

He was still holding the baby when the phone buzzed suddenly. He didn't check it immediately.

Who is it anyway? he wondered. He remembered that he came back here because he believed that he would find an atmosphere of revelry. This time he hoped that he might find the baby boy's mother but couldn't. He stepped inside the house like the previous time, this time without knocking. *What if someone is hiding in here? he* thought bluntly. But he felt he would eventually find Fefe. He felt a great relief. But he must get home quickly and see his other friends. He wanted to get to Alex and party but it was impossible. This was a chance, a desperate chance, and he had taken it. That mattered to him the most as he left the house in a hurry.

He didn't realise that he was about to run into a group of protesters in the driveway. They were protesting against the municipality's lack of service delivery. His eyes sensed the danger but couldn't go out to the street because he might put himself in danger. Besides, he was afraid of the police vehicles. He must have waited there for about twenty minutes, all the while watching what was hap-pening in the streets.

The hum and buzz so common in Ramaphosa Street rose to a crescendo. It was so savage, so cold-blooded, so frightening. He still held the baby in his hands. For a moment, he thought about leaving the baby there and driving away. It would be simple for him. Yes, just leave the baby behind and he would be free of this burden. After all, it was not his child.

The police vehicles were moving up and down the street and he wondered if it would be fair to just leave the baby there alone outside the house. He took a deep breath and exhaled softly. Not his of course. This thought reminded him that he had done this because the baby wasn't his. It was not theirs. This specific incident had initially started here and he knew that the baby wasn't his. So why did they kidnap him in the first place? He felt he must get home soon because the baby wasn't his.

Suddenly, he began to squat there like an outlaw because the baby wasn't his. Why didn't he leave him here even though he had previously tried to keep the baby? He knew he was going to be in big trouble. He licked his dry lips and couldn't put him the down on the ground. He looked at the noisy crowd and wanted to get into the vehicle. Then the wild primitive determination rose in him, the blind determination to go through with a task once begun whether it can be avoided in time or not, whether the angry crowd could be dangerous to him or not. *No*, he thought accurately. He was not going to part with the baby.

What if it was his baby boy? Was he going to leave him here alone and be vulnerable to the murderers of the world? Or would he take off with the baby and redevelop the forgotten mercy again? He remembered how much he liked to talk to Fefe when she was still around and wondered why she hadn't called him for so long.

He tried to keep away from his notorious friends but that was not easy to do. He was a handsome man and even the most beautiful chased after him over the years. He remembered Fefe from when they saw her at her house. He didn't care much about her aunt even till today. His main concern was the mother of the child. The baby boy. But his anxious regression didn't really mean he had gotten away with the crime because he hadn't given up on finding Eliot. It felt like Eliot had been owing them a lot. Yet, he had been a ladies' man and had a house in Centurion.

By then, he was the perfect family man and it was difficult to believe how many beautiful women he had been involved in over the years. Still, there was something fatherly and human about him. At times, he thought about adopting the baby so that he could belong to him eternally. But that wasn't going to be possible. Instead, he could be taken to prison for kidnapping the child and his other crimes would come to light. He cared about the children from poor neighbourhoods though. Often, he bought them food and clothes with his own money.

He wondered how many people they had kidnapped before, especially from Zola and Tembisa. He wondered what he could do or say if he was ordered by his bosses to kidnap the children from his own neighbourhood. How could he do it? How could he live there together with their parents and how would he face them? He thought and swallowed hard. He had been fabulously admired all the people in his neighbourhood, including the kids.

On one occasion, he had taken them to the zoo. It was an unforgettable experience. He didn't like it when he had to go back to his criminal life. He had just left his wife and children at home and had promised to be right back. He wouldn't leave the baby behind. He felt like it was now his and Fefe's. He was going to fly to KwaZulu Natal and come back but at the same time, he knew things would get more complicated than he had anticipated.

All he wanted was to feel the fresh air and travel the world. He had finally given up on returning home. He urged his wife to come to the hotel but she wanted to stop by in Durban for a few days, as planned. His wife didn't want to disappoint him and her children. However, she had a strange feeling about travelling further and suddenly suggested not to go anywhere. They had remained there in Durban and she promised to be with him the following day.

However, he realised that someone had been following him but wasn't sure who the person was. He was a hulk of a man. He wore dark glasses and a black leather jacket. That alone intimidated him somewhat. He was considering taking a flight on South African Airways or another airline when he got a call from Fefe. She told him that the police had been looking for him and that she wanted to see her baby boy. She said she missed him more than anything in this world. He had been like a zombie for days, unable to believe that the police were after him. Still, they couldn't track him down because they didn't know where he was. As for the baby. Why didn't Fefe tell him this before?

Unfortunately, twelve dangerous terrorists had boarded the plane and blown it up. Everyone on board died. Having heard the terrible news Fefe couldn't believe that that could happen to her baby and the hitman. She kept on thinking that if she had reported the matter to the police earlier, the situation could have been prevented. The 'if only' of that day had haunted her for days, for months and years. The facial expressions from the police had actually told her that something had gone wrong even before they broke the news themselves to the family.

Mandla was in prison as he had been arrested for a crime he had committed together with his friends from Mamelodi, Pretoria. And as time went on, Fefe fell ill from what had happened. It was a nightmare from which she had thought she would not awake from. All she wanted was to be together with her baby. She didn't care that the hitman had died; to her, he deserved it. She could not forget her baby and the manner in which he had been killed.

Sometimes, she had nightmares about the flight and she hadn't gone anywhere for years ever since her baby died. She wanted to blame Eliot for everything that had happened. All of it. But then there was no recapturing the past. There was no turning back. She felt that her baby boy was irreplaceable but she knew he would not come back to life. It was the kind of thing one reads about in the news but it had happened to her. She felt as though her whole family had been wiped out by the same dangerous thugs. In some ways, she felt like her life would never be the same again. She wished she hadn't met Eliot and the drug dealers. She had hated all the drug lords and the state.

Every time she saw the village children playing around together, she would observe them keenly. But they were not hers. And her baby would never exist again. There would never be another baby like him in her entire life and she wanted to be there for him. She lived with his memories right up till this very day.

She saw other children every day but they were not like her son. She knew it would take time to forget him. She knew that she should carry on with her life and that there were other men out there. She had only had one serious relationship. She had never married and knew she never would but had no reason not to. She felt she had had it all at one time but lost it all. It made her philosophical about life and she wouldn't commit suicide like others had done. But a piece of her heart had died with her baby. How everything had changed.

Her aunt had gone from her life to another place with her husband-to-be. She was gone, probably for good. She called her twice to apologise for leaving in such a hurry. She didn't return her call. Still, she missed her aunt, her baby, her entire life.

On that night, the township of Tembisa was quiet and there was no loadshedding. She lifted her eyes towards the moonlit sky and breathed slowly. Now that she had lost her baby, it didn't matter how long she stayed like that. *Where was God in all of this?* she wondered bitterly. Everyone who had ever mattered to her believed in God. Even the hitmen. But was she supposed to connect with that God when she wanted to? The man she used to love was out of her life forever and she still yearned to see him. Just to see him. Although he wasn't the father of her dead child, he reminded her of her baby boy. She remembered that they had come a very long way together.

But what was she supposed to do in the meantime? Why can't she just forget him and allow him to continue with the woman with albinism? She wondered what could have happened if they had any children together. But why can't she focus on her current husband-to-be? She thought, feeling devastated. What she knew was that she had to meet Eliot even in death.

The breeze was cold against her face but she didn't care. She had been driven by memories of life. No matter how Eliot had messed up with her one truth seemed to resonate in her heart. God had never denied or neglected her. She had lost everyone who had mattered to her and all of them had an amazing faith. Besides, they were so kind and brilliant. But she wondered if God had genuinely loved her. If he had been on her side. *No, God has never been on my side*, she thought to herself.

Even so, she still felt lost and even questioned if God truly existed and whether it actually mattered how a person lived their life. The most important thing for her was why most people would always put their faith and hope in a God they had never known or seen with their own eyes.

Why were most blinded by the same God who had helped them even in death sometimes? Then, one day, Fefe decided to call Eliot. This time he answered her. She told him about the tragic death of her son and he humbly said he was extremely sorry for what happened. And besides, he had never known about it until much later. If he had been so much concerned about her that way, then why didn't he call her all these years?

She then asked him about the whereabouts of the albino woman but he didn't answer. He didn't want to because he was scared that the police and the Nigerian men were still after him. He knew he couldn't tell her where he was now living. He couldn't just trust anyone. Besides, he thought that she might have been sent to find him.

After all these years, he and Sophie had two children, a three-year-old boy and a one-year-old girl. He was now happy that someone had finally come into his life and given him the love and devotion he deserved. Not the unnecessary lies. He stared at the wall in the house as they spoke on the phone, then snapped it shut and slipped it into his trousers pocket. From the moment he had heard about the baby's death, he didn't feel well just like the previous time.

He felt guilty and thought that if he had been there for Fefe, none of this would have happened. He wondered what he should do to calm her down. What he should have done to prove her wrong? But he knew very well that he couldn't risk his life by going back there.

He still wasn't done with his French Revolution assignment. The desire for him to go to France was something that he still owed to himself and his ancestors. He felt he should go together with his sweetheart and children. And he couldn't wait. However, for now, the timing was bad. It had been raining heavily and there was a lot of traffic.

For weeks and months, Eliot couldn't stop thinking about the death of Fefe's son. He felt as though he had acted wrongfully by running away with or without the woman. He stupidly spent the next few days talking to himself about the ways he could have saved the little boy's life. He had mixed emotions. He had told his darling about what was eating him lately. Then suddenly she grinned and slipped her arm around Eliot's shoulders and hands. That's what he loved, the feeling of her hands in his. Especially now as things have been sour recently. Still, she missed her home and ever since they had run away together, she had never returned to her home.

What if her mom too had now passed away because of her disappearance? Finally, in the early autumn, she decided to go back home. Eliot decided to stay where he was out of fear that people were still looking for him. He told her that if anyone asked about his whereabouts, she should tell them that he had died two years ago. He told her to only tell the truth to her mom and anyone else that she genuinely trusted.

CHAPTER
Seven

Sophie had been homesick for quite a while now and her mom had been very pleased that she had returned home. Though she had been warmly welcomed, she did not receive a heroin's welcome. No press photographers, no former headmasters to welcome the return of the prodigal daughter. Only her mother and all other family members were there, exuding a generous eagerness and haste. Her two children also received a kind welcome and unconditional love for the first time ever. "Why did you take so long to come back home, my daughter? Where did you disappear to?" her mom asked desperately. She looked like she wanted to cry. They were having a good conversation at home in the dining room. All the family members were watching and listening while Sophie answered. "It was so difficult Mom."

"What do you mean my dear?"
"I was kidnapped Mom."
"Who did that?"
"Eliot."

"Who's Eliot?" her mother asked. Sophie tried explaining briefly to her mom and eventually, she wept tearfully and was given a piece of white cloth to wipe her face. But her innocent falling tears were welling down her face like an angry waterfall. But she wiped it out at last. "What did you do in Roodepoort for so long Sophie?" her mother asked. "Travelled," Sophie replied. "For ten years?" "Yes, of course, Mom. But at least I survived the kidnapping and so on. Maybe if it wasn't for Eliot, I would have most certainly been murdered for rituals. Her mother looked at her face while she spoke. Her kids were pinkish just like herself and the whole family. "Many people would be glad to see you alive again," her mother said. "How are they now?" "Fine. But Nunu, a retired medical doctor, died two years ago now. She suddenly fell ill" But the rebuke in Sophie's voice didn't escape her. Her whole family including her siblings were not disappointed in her for they had always suspected that there might be something wrong that happened to Sophie and that she wouldn't disappear for no reason. They were fully aware that the kidnapping of people with albinism was a regular occurrence and the government had done nothing to prevent that evil

Most villagers had been looking at her and her kids since she had arrived. That afternoon she stood on the stoep, feeling lost, despite her being homesick, despite her experience, despite the immunity she had acquired to physical change. But the valley was gone. Above all, the village was still the same before she was kidnapped. When Eliot had asked her to return to Roodepoort she had refused. But she had no real reason to do that, however, ever since she had returned home, she wanted to be there alone with her family members. But after a while, she had courteously asked him to come over. He was the father of their kids after all, so she couldn't lose him for anything. Besides, she was alive today all because of his kindness and humanity.

Coming from a very poor background, he had learnt a lot from the rough life he experienced in the past. He learnt other things from Raphael, the Nigerian boss, apart from hiding his feelings when denied something he desperately wanted. He had been disappointed a lot by the African National Congress and the government due to corruption. He was denied the promised general work he had volunteered for. He had learnt the freedom of uncombed hair, that poverty was freedom to a child for whom in manhood, even liberty would be impoverished.

Most of all, he learnt that poverty would lead some to an unexpected world. To hell. That freedom itself grew up on an empty stomach like a stunted flower and took the kidnapping to nowhere. At last, even though he had doubts, Eliot decided to go to Sophie's family home. He had honestly asked for forgiveness from her family for kidnapping her all those years ago. Although he had done so, it was hard for them to believe that he had totally changed and that he wouldn't do the same thing again. Once a thug always a thug, isn't it? What if he told his friends to kidnap other members of the family? On the other hand, what if he was the person God sent to protect them from other possible crimes?

After a few days, he was becoming used to this village and he liked it as long as his darling was beside him. One morning while in the bedroom with Sophie he slowly smiled at her over the coffee. He remembered the tragedy in Fefe's baby's life. He wondered if he was among the dead victims now. It had been a long time but still, he didn't wear it on his sleeve. He never talked about Fefe or her relatives, except to very close childhood friends. Everybody had been devastated by the victims' deaths.

There had been a memorial service at Fefe's home that had been attended by many people. However, the had been no funeral because there were no bodies for the airline to return. There had been nothing at all. Only air. And heartbreak. And the broken memories. And the regrets. Sometimes, Eliot wanted to put all that mess upon his shoulders. He had wanted to blame himself for the plane crash and that he should have saved that baby.

"How can Shotgun do all this?" he said referring to himself but at the same time, he was talking to his Sophie, who had been looking at him with misery. He had heard more than that. It had dismally occurred, according to him. However, he had to focus on his current affairs. Sophie was his main priority. He knew what she was capable of. He wanted to marry her. He exactly knew who and what she was. He had wanted to surprise her. It was her presence and her beauty that brought him to life now. Her soft voice and respect for him.

Still, he wanted to make the plane crash his own business. He had lived with that tragedy as though it was his loss for a long time. He had put it aside and even made peace with it. It no longer ruled his life. Only Sophie's love did and he liked that and he was thinking about that now. He thought about the wedding arrangements and when it should take place. He still had enough cash and was not ready to return to crime.

His previous criminal activities made him feel like he wasn't human. That he lived a fake life. But he knew that their relationship had to be kept a secret. When he was out at his house they did not usually meet as he didn't like leaving his house alone. Ever since their departure, it had been vandalised and all the windows had been broken.

All this had created the broken memories between himself and Fefe.

He remembered the day when he was on the road to France and how concerned he was about the real effects of the French Revolution. Whenever he and Sophie telephoned each other, they would return the receiver to its cradle if someone other than them lifted it at the other end. And whenever they arranged to go to the cinema, they would enter separately. Occasionally, they met in the inner city and took the bus to the Zoo Lake. Why didn't he buy a nice vehicle?

They would sit down beside the lake and look at the birds nesting in the trees on the islet in the middle or at the swans floating past or walking on the wide stretches of lawn shaded by pines and oaks. But their main problem, according to Sophie's family, was the greatest disparity between them. Their true love was blind and flowing. At the lake, they sat under the green tree, far away from other groups. They sat there, having some drinks and stuff, and they talked for a while. She sat there next to him and walked with him holding his hand as he looked at her face.

For three weeks he had been alone in his house without her. Yet she couldn't write or call him these days. "How could she have forgotten me?" he asked himself as he stood on the front porch, looking far into the space. Sometimes he felt like she didn't love him anymore. Or it was that she had enough of the situation? He realised that he would have a huge problem living without her. But Fefe sometimes had given him a headache.

When she told him that she still had feelings for him and that she was ready to have children together with him, he wasn't interested. He told her he would think about it. She knew he was trying to avoid her. What she knew was that she was going to teach him a better lesson if he had totally declined her request. "But you know that I have someone else right?" Eliot said as he stood alone at the front porch staring into space. He usually enjoyed listening to the singing birds and he believed that it was a sign of peace of mind for himself. He wondered what he would do if his past accomplices found. He seemed not to trust Fefe the most and that she could sell him out for the lost love.

But why didn't she continue with the person she was in love with before? Why had she become a burden lately? He thought grimly. "But you know that I love you Eliot!" Fefe said almost in tears. She was more than desperate for him to love her back. If not, he had to die so that no one else could have him. He didn't like her to argue with him or to whine.

Every time she talked about it, he felt unhappy. And when he refused to be in love with her again she promised to bring the kidnappers into his house. As a result, he was left trembling. The more he thought about that, the more he kept trembling uncontrollably. He knew that she was creating a joke out of nothing. He had always known how dangerous jealousy could be especially if someone has fallen out of love. He really felt threatened by this woman, but why didn't he relocate somewhere where he could always be free? But why should he be murdered or die for the lost love? Why didn't he go and pay a visit to France and stop thinking about something that couldn't benefit him? This was a real moment of total distraction.

He wished he had the wisdom to realise this in the better days with her. Why didn't she understand that Eliot had moved on with his own life? He thought bluntly. Thinking about Fefe made him uneasy. He wondered where she was and what was she planning against him. He knew how dangerous the kidnappers were and it wasn't something to play with. He switched off his cell phone and left it on the couch. He was in the bedroom when he heard a knock at the front door. It startled him.

It was eight o'clock in the evening when he was alarmed by the knock. He could hear the murmur of men's voices. He couldn't make out their words but he picked their brisk official tone. Were these the usual guys from the village? He wasn't sure. He sat at the edge of the bed, completely still. Then, he heard the kitchen door open. There was complete silence. He peered through the cubicle and realised that there was someone there but didn't know who it was.

"Who is it?" he asked.

The guys said nothing and two of them were still outside the door. He wanted to run, intended to flee and he knew that he was going to make use of the back door if things happened to get bad. He peered out the bedroom door and he saw the same man loitering around the kitchen and he realised that the thug couldn't see him. He wondered if he heard his voice when he called out loudly. There was a squeak of different shoes now on the floor and a rustle of clothes. Then he bent down to avoid the shooting in case there was any. He was too afraid to walk to the criminals across the floor, push open the kitchen room door and flee. He knew it would be dangerous.

Who were these guys and what were they looking for? When he saw that they were heavily armed, he decided to escape through the bedroom window. He closed it slowly after he had climbed out. He was free to escape but he knew he had to be careful. Who sent these guys to look for him?

"Where are you Eliot?" one of them yelled, holding a gun in his hand. The predators were intending to shoot him dead. That's what they were sent to do to him. All of them were now inside the house and searching desperately for Eliot. There were the sounds of rattling and movement in the house and then silence. Eliot was outside and decided to hide under an old car without wheels that had been there for decades.

Realising that he wasn't in, they couldn't decide to leave. It had been an hour since they entered the house. They thought that they would find him. Didn't they hear his voice as soon as they had come into the yard? Fifteen minutes passed, half an hour and more than an hour or so. Then the loadshedding began and the lights went off abruptly. The darkness was absolute. They went outside to look for him but there was complete darkness and silence.

Eliot contemplated coming out from under the vehicle. He was safe there for now but what if he was discovered and shot? How would he make it to France for the interview? When he heard the voices outside for a moment he was frightened. It was as though some great catastrophe had occurred while he was under the car. It was as if the car had been buried or destroyed in a silent earthquake or gas attack that had somehow left him untouched.

But then he heard a texture in the silence, humming and muffled, a rustling undercurrent. Yes, it was still dark in and outside the house. And everywhere. But there was nothing wrong with it. Why would Fefe be after his life if he had stopped loving her? Hiding under the vehicle, he felt half-freed. And half depressed. But he wasn't sure when they would go away. He wondered where his wife was and wished they were together by now, making love. He wondered if she had known that he was in trouble. He realised that he had gotten himself into a serious problem but he had to wait for the right time for them to leave. They had stupidly thought that he had run away immediately when they had arrived.

There was something else that had almost told them that Eliot was still around. The winds were blowing uncontrollably from the west and a thunderstorm struck suddenly. The guys preferred to wait outside on the front porch and play for time. When Eliot wanted to move from the safety of being und the car, three shots were fired into the dark sky. They couldn't really think that Eliot was under the old vehicle. This vehicle was old and had once belonged to his late uncle from Kimberly who used to work at Eskom.

They still waited there in front of the house but a vehicle couldn't tell them anything. Yet their deadly intention was unspeakable. The moment that another vehicle of theirs had arrived Eliot knew that he was in danger. Through the car's lights, he noticed two young men approaching their accomplices who were waiting in the yard. It was a thing he had talked about, now he was to see it for himself. He realised the impending danger. His mouth was dry, his heart was pounding in his chest and something within him was weeping out in protest against the pending death event.

Who made these guys aware that I had returned home? he thought. Suddenly, he heard the sound of their steps getting closer. But the guys seemed to talk for a while before searching the entire yard for him. His fear was great and instant; the smell of it went from his body to the nostrils. At that very moment, one of them spoke and gave them directions. Another gunshot again but he couldn't do anything. He couldn't move an inch.

The old vehicle's wheels had been replaced by four dark bricks. He fell into some grotesque shape of wire which was barbed and tore at his clothes and flesh. Then it held him so that he thought that death was near. He felt hopeless. Even now the guys couldn't talk to each other but wondered where he might have been. Yes, the ruthless death was next to him, and for the moment the injustices of life filled him with anger.

He lay there for a moment expecting the blow that would end him, but his wits came to him and he turned twice but was under the car. The dead car of course. He wondered if he could manage to fly to France at last now that he was under siege. Can he amend the issues of the French Revolution? Who was Louis XIV and how old would he be today? If Louis XIV was still alive today, would he be allowed to talk to him?

As arrogant as he was, wasn't he going to beat him up and say he was up to something? He thought while he was under the vehicle. Where were the villagers and why didn't they come out to help him? Who was ready to be shot to death by these guys? His heart was like a wild thing in his chest and seemed to lift his whole body each time that it beat. He tried to calm his heartbeat down out of fear that they might hear him along with the noise of his gasping breath but he couldn't.

It was raining heavily but the guys were not prepared to leave without finding Eliot. Did he learn the final lesson today? That he should never trust a woman? Any woman at all? But can Fefe do that to him? Will she be happy to see him dead? How many men have been murdered by their wives in different marriages? How many men have died because of their innocent and stupid love affairs?

"Let's go gents," one of them said eventually. The rain had stopped and he could hear them speaking to each other as they left the yard.

At last, he got out from under the vehicle. He was tired of being under the vehicle with rusty wires on it. He ran away to another area in Alex. He won't forget what had happened to him in his own home. But can he forgive Fefe for what had happened to him? For what she did to him?

<h1 style="text-align:center">C H A P T E R
 Eight</h1>

It had been three weeks since Eliot's home had been left stranded. The house was deserted. Almost all the doors had been left open but the neighbourhood wasn't too concerned. Eliot wanted to go back home and check out what was happening there. He wanted to approach Fefe to find out what had happened. Fefe missed him. She missed the touch of his hand, his laugh, his smile when he said her name.

She wished he should have come back into her life, their whole life. Missing him was good, but then she felt the usual pang of regret that she couldn't be there or hadn't been there when he needed her, especially after his attempt to visit France. But this time the feeling of regret was over-shadowed by what she had done to him. If she really wanted to get back to their old life or revise their relationship, she wasn't sure if it was what he wanted to do. He wanted to blame her but on the other hand, there was nothing more he had wanted from her, unless he kept the secret love for her, that he wouldn't want Sophie to find out about that. Otherwise, he would have ruined almost everything, the trust and honesty he had usually talked about. But that's what Fefe had to say to him when he found her at Alex. "I've missed you," she told him. "You missed me?" he asked with the innocent curiosity. The way he said it was as if he had explained everything. He wanted her to believe him and to give in but it wasn't enough.

"I've missed your true love. I know that I was wrong to send out the hitmen to your house," Fefe said. He was becoming more indignant with a feeling of reproach. But there was also a feeling of love left as well, just a little bit of it. The one that she had ruined by falling pregnant from someone else. The one whom she had totally forgotten by now. The main one that she didn't want to see any longer for Eliot's love.

Eliot had to listen to her story though as she went on to say, "I've missed you so much. I've missed our conversations. I've missed everything about you. I've missed hearing your name on my lips. I've missed seeing you smile when I walk into a room. Mostly, I've missed the taste of your mouth, the touch of your hand." Then she lifted his hand to her lips and kissed his fingertips. Wasn't what she had always wanted from the start? She had known very well that the albino woman had been her whole distraction in her life.

"Alright, I heard you out... So, you love me?" he said once again. But she continued to say, "Yes of course I do. I want to be the best woman I can be. For you." She held him in his arms and revelled in the sensation of having him pressed against her. They talked about everything that happened in her life including the death of her baby, but he didn't want to talk about that.

The main reason that he had come here was because he wanted to create a peaceful relationship between himself and Fefe. In addition, he wanted her to stop what she had been doing. He wanted her to stop sending the hitmen to his house and to make sure that he was always safe even when he had returned from France. He also wanted to ensure that his sweetheart Sophie would be safe. After all, she was the mother of his children. But he didn't know that Fefe's jealousy would create another problem one day. She had wanted to totally destroy the relationship between him and Sophie because she believed that they would be happily married one day. She loathed the fact that he had children with that woman. Sometimes she felt as though she was useless because she failed him, she failed herself.

"I want you to know that you will always be my best man in the world. That I can even give up everything for you.

I want to be always with you alone. But I want to ask you to give me another chance. Can you do that for me?" she pleaded.

He hesitated. She had been wondering the same thing herself just moments before. He wasn't expecting her to say that. Or to be more accurate it wasn't what he had hoped for. When he went to sit outside under the tree she didn't hesitate to join him and she knew it was because she was eager to have just one moment with him. It didn't mean that she would be happy for the casual relationship, hence she wanted to overtake that albino woman.

She had known very well what she would do to win this man over forever. That she wouldn't mind sending the hitmen again to kill that woman. Then it means that she would have won triumphantly. But that would be unfair, for God's sake. Do you think she would have cared about that? First of all, why didn't he stop coming here? How can he prevent the woman's life as promised? The only woman he loved with his whole heart.

But Fefe was on her way. She only wanted to have all of him, emotionally, and physically. If not, she was better off alone. She really didn't want a casual relationship; she yearned for something deeper. But how can he let her make the unnecessary demands on him? Everything they had discussed was important but still, it didn't get him any closer to knowing what he needed to know. He felt he had talked about everything but nothing because they didn't talk about his Sophie. And he needed to know if there could be a 'them' in his heart. He knew that he shouldn't have been here, but for safety's sake, it was good.

He suddenly stood up and led her into the bedroom where she allowed him to sit down on the side of the bed while he watched her stand in front of him. Then she put her arms around his neck. She leaned her head on his shoulder as they spoke. She wanted to know when he would go to France and he responded that he wasn't sure. There was no reason why he should do that together with her, while Sophie might be looking for him. Of course, she missed him badly. She wondered why he didn't even call. He hadn't even written her letters to inspire her. Sometimes she wondered what type of man he was. She still had time to learn about him, about men. But Fefe, on the other hand, was happy to be with him. She hoped he would give her Sophie's address.

"Can you please go with me," she said softly. She had been wearing flat shoes earlier that day.

It wasn't that cold outside so the bedroom window was wide open. The curtains had been shifted sideways. But she already knew why she demanded that they should go away to France. There was a silent but desperate reason and still, he wasn't aware what was it or why. He should be very careful of being blinded by love, blinded by her soft voice and her crocodile smile. Did he know that lately, she was more dangerous than he had ever known?

"Really?" he asked with a wide smile. But she felt short in front of him. Her jealousy was much deeper than anything, it was deeper than the Indian Ocean. Although he wasn't married, he still had to learn more about women, especially this one. Even now she wanted all of him. She wanted him to love her, only her and not any other woman. She was greedy and selfish. Meanwhile, he had just agreed that they would fly together to France. She was happy upon hearing that. Little did she know, he was lying to her.

The following day he went to town alone and bought her a magnificent diamond necklace. She wanted it so desperately that her heart began to thump. Initially, he didn't tell her that it was hers or he had bought it for her. He had just shown it to her and smiled. It was as though she had already known that it belonged to her. So when he said, "It's all yours," her hands were shaking as she picked it up. She put it around her neck over her high blouse and stood in ecstasy before her reflection in the glass. She couldn't believe that he had bought it for her.

"Are you sure that you bought it for me my love?" she asked hesitantly, her anxiety showing in her voice. She frantically thought he might change his mind. But he couldn't do that.

"Yes of course," he replied. Then she threw her arms around his neck like the previous time and kissed him wildly with treasure. She felt as though she had triumphed. On the other hand, he knew that he was supposed to leave but couldn't. She was wearing it, her pair of bright heels and the white long, smart dress. She had a better intention for that. At that moment, she was the prettiest woman in the house, elegant, graceful, smiling in the seventh heaven of happiness.

In the township of Alex, all the men looked at her chokingly and wanted to know her better. They wanted to be introduced to her. Most young men wanted to get closer to her and Eliot didn't like it. He had become somewhat jealous of her and the way she looked, He wondered if he should fly away together with her. But she smiled with love and was wrapped in a cloud of happiness, the results of all the daily compliments, all the administration. All these awakened a desire to fly to France more than anything. It could have been a wonderful success so dear to every woman's heart.

A few weeks later, he received a call from Sophie who was missing him terribly. Every time she called Fefe had stupidly become angry. She couldn't control her jealousy and sometimes she cried loudly so that he felt pity for her. But she knew what her intention had been.

Every time Sophie Fefe would automatically say, "What is it this time? What does she want now? Can't she understand that you are now with me?" She would say hateful words, words that sometimes made him feel sick. Those were unforgettable and sometimes he felt like she should just go away and never come back here.

But when the hitmen had called on her phone she lied to him that it was just someone else she knew. But, when the number of calls continued he became stupidly jealous too. Wasn't that what she had wanted all along? Of course, that was what she had wanted him to be. For her alone. Rubbish! After that what was he going to benefit? What must he do with Sophie?

"You know I love you so much Eliot. And I don't know what I would be without you," she told him one day. He wasn't expecting to hear that. The bedroom had been so quiet and lonely. *If I wasn't around with her what would have happened in this cold bedroom today?* he thought.

"I love you too," he replied as he smiled. He grinned at her, his expression alive with love, hope and adoration that had been there since the day he wanted to leave. The day when he bought her a magnificent diamond. He brushed his hand along the back of her head.

"I want us to make children, children of our own. Please love," she said. When he nodded in approval it was as though he had already known what she was going to say. He scanned her, looking as happy as he had been when they had first met. He crooked his finger and placed it beneath her chin.

"Darling, I'm so desperate about my plea right now." He suddenly brought his lips closer to hers and kissed her slowly, tenderly. It was as though they had started kissing ever since their relationship had developed.

"But will you love me the way I do?" she asked one more time and watched him closely. Then Eliot returned the warm kiss, amazed at the passion between them that day. He wished there wouldn't be unnecessary wars between them ever again. Then she eased back, her voice huskier than before.

"But you know that I love you so much baby."

But she wouldn't want to know what he was thinking. Of course, it was about the woman he left behind. Still, he wasn't sure about having kids with Fefe. He wanted to but there was no guarantee that it would really happen. *Otherwise, it should have happened long ago. Isn't it?* he thought, but he couldn't tell her about what had just come into his mind. For he knew that she would be hurt. It was just a feeling, not quite a decision.

They were quiet for a second. Finally, Eliot had stopped kissing her. And he faced her. He looked around the bedroom and then looked through the window. It was about to rain when she got another call that minute. She knew that he hated it and he stood up, feeling irritated. But there was nothing he could do because she still lied to him and this time she said it was her aunt who happened to miss her. It was still the same men. She didn't say anything in front of him or otherwise, she would lose him.

But why didn't she tell them to leave her alone if she was really serious about this relationship? Besides, she had wishes and demands for him. His eyes found hers and for the first time in a long time, she saw something other than the easy-going confidence and love looking back at her. But there was something else that he didn't quite understand about her. Why was it that every time they had a conversation, she became frightened like a chicken when she got a call? Why? What had gone wrong with her?

"You know, I will always love you more than the previous time baby. My love for you is immeasurable and amazing. Right?" She smiled again uncontrollably. She felt a sense of alarm but she didn't blink and didn't want to miss whatever was coming.

But why had he decided to spend more time here together with this lady while Sophie was looking for him? Also, Sophie was pregnant again and she needed him by her side. She wanted to touch him again and feel the taste of his mouth like be. She wanted to be touched by him and for him to make her feel special.

He was certain that he would ultimately return to Sophie. She told him that she was pregnant and he knew the child was his. So, he had become more frustrated than before and wasn't sure if he could manage to make babies with Fefe. Yet he didn't say anything more than he had just said. He kissed her again, longer this time.

She wasn't thinking about the pending call, about him. Not even a little. But still, he couldn't make promises about the future. Everything about their relationship had taught them that much. They had come a long way together. And she understood very well what he meant and how he was feeling. Everything about life as they had known was supposed to have changed by now. He was supposed to give her more attention but Sophie was still in the picture. Even though there would be days when they wouldn't see each other, she was still his girl-friend. He thought so.

That night she didn't get any more calls from anyone. Or didn't she get it from her aunt either? While in the bed-room, he placed his hands on her face and kissed her slowly for a long time. When he pulled back, the love in his expression was so pure and real and deep, it took her breath away.

"How much you love me Eliot?" she asked emotionally and she knew she couldn't control the love that had developed within her veins at that moment. That was the sort of love Eliot had longed for, a sort of love she wasn't even sure that she would one day achieve. The rainy nights she had desperately prayed about it, asking the almighty God if a love like this one existed and if He could please move mountains just so she could experience it.

CHAPTER
Nine

Now that he had been here for long, Eliot must have brought happiness and warmth. But after nine months, he vanished once again. He couldn't tell Fefe that he was planning on leaving as he had known that she would be stubborn and wouldn't allow him to go away.

He left about four in the morning when she was still in bed, snoring harmoniously. She had been dozing since midnight in that small bedroom and that wasn't what she had anticipated. He was gone forever and had no intention of returning. He left immediately after she got a call from Sophie to inform him that she had given birth to a handsome baby boy and that she named him Eliyah.

When Fefe had woken up she had been conscious of all this and she therefore hurried to the taxi rank to look for him. She didn't know what had happened to him or where he had gone too. Why didn't he inform her that he was leaving? She returned to the house and searched everywhere for him but he wasn't there. She was dumbfounded.

"Where is this man?" she asked herself painfully. She went down the street in search of him. For her, it felt as though it was the end of something and she remembered that she had to be there at home at eight. Suddenly, she broke into tears. The man she loved was gone, no doubt about that.

"Did he really love me?" she asked herself. She was still in disbelief and the anger inside her was unbearable. She went back into the bedroom and looked for him once again. He wasn't there. She searched the other bedroom but there was no sign of him. She was utterly crushed. That night she remained in her evening dress, without the strength even to go to bed, collapsed on a chair, without a fire, her mind blank. She had gone out looking for him in the neighbourhood and returned around ten. She had found nobody.

The following day she had gone out to the police station to report the matter and also to offer a reward that could give her a flicker of hope about Eliot's whereabouts. She waited all day but there was no news. She returned home in the evening, her face pale and lined. She had discovered nothing. What she wanted was Eliot and nobody else. She wanted him and she knew that she would not give up on him. Otherwise...

She suspected that he had gone away to be that bastard. She was furious. Then, she remembered that he had given her the address where Sophie and her family were living. Sometimes when she was at home, she would sit down near the window and dream of that day long ago after Eliot had disappeared.

What would have happened to him if he didn't go to Sophie's place? Who can say? She felt a wave of emotion come over her. When she asked him to come back over the phone he said he would but at the moment he was still busy at Sophie's place. When asked if they would still fly to France together, he said he wasn't sure about that. When asked if he would fly together with Sophie he became quiet, not knowing what to say anymore.

She longed to go to France with Eliot. She also wanted to know more about the French Revolution from its government. She couldn't wait to fly there with him. However, if he disappointed her again, then Sophie would have to be kidnapped and murdered. She had remembered that she could live without him and he knew that. But the matter right now was whether Eliot would choose Sophie or Fefe to accompany him when he eventually takes that flight to France.

It had been too much now and when she finally wanted to know if he would fly to France with her, he said no because there wasn't enough money. That was a lie. However, Eliot had made a big mistake by telling her where Sophie and her family lived. At times, he didn't feel safe but he couldn't say it. He knew what Fefe would do to him and Sophie herself was already affected.

"I will have to teach him a lesson, one way or another." she said to herself one day and continued in vernacular language, "*Akandazi kakuhle uEliot.*"

A great weariness enveloped her. She hadn't eaten almost the whole day and the thought of food made her feel sick. The dark clouds in the atmosphere gathered together and there was a better hope for the daily rain. But the last thing she needed was to die from shock and hunger. She had learnt a lot about the difficulties of love. That life wasn't as easy as she had thought it to be. But seeing her standing in the doorway had been the most horrible moment of her life.

She felt a cold sweat wash over her at the memory. She was very angry with almost everybody in the township and with herself. She was taking it out on herself as though it was her fault that he was gone. For three nights she switched on the bedroom light and lamp in the dining room and read *Othello*. If Eliot came home tonight she would be elated, and if she goes away again she will possibly be damned. she thought worriedly.

How easy it was for him to lie that he loved me, she thought to herself in disgust. She couldn't stand the pain and wanted control over the subject matter. She read the book until she was tired and nearly fell asleep. Then, she stood up and went to the kitchen to make a cup of coffee. She was wound tight with nerves, half expecting to hear a knock at the door. She wondered if he would really leave her behind and go to France. Would he really choose Sophie over her?

Didn't he have real feelings for her anyway? Didn't she know that he had a wife-to-be and Sophie was having a baby boy? What would happen if he didn't come back? What would happen if he came back tomorrow? If he comes home tomorrow. What was Fefe feeling now? Did she feel guilty that he was gone and that she wouldn't see the future in France? Why didn't she call Mandla, the father of her late baby boy? But, how would that be possible if he was still in prison? *But even if he was out, he's useless,* she thought angrily.

She viciously thought that Eliot would be sorry for what he did to her. She hoped he would suffer. She wanted him to suffer the consequences of his wrongdoings. She hated him for leaving her again. She felt as though she had been fooled. She would make him pay for the rest of his life for what he had done to her. She was going to make sure he was dead or something. That his dignity would be rags and tatters. But can she really find peace and happiness over this?

CHAPTER
Ten

Fefe was still sad. The past Friday she had nearly told the hitmen Sophie's address but something must have stopped her miraculously. But she was supposed to have done that of course. For Sophie and Eliot, life was going to be fucking gruesome for the foreseeable future. In addition, she was going to insist that he stop seeing Sophie.

But how can he do that? Above all, Sophie was the mother of his children. She didn't know that he could. She thought that maybe they ease off for a while and when Fefe's heat had died down, they would get back together. Or if he had chosen Fefe for the possible visit to France, then everything might go as smoothly as he wanted. But that wasn't possible, what was the use of daydreaming?

In other words, she wanted him. She wanted to force him to choose to be with her but she felt bewildered, angry and lost. But why want to put pressure on him, knowing that it was the worst thing that she could do? She decided to call the hitmen but they were not available and asked her to call at another time.

Why did she want to avenge him and the innocent albino woman for the lost love? Why didn't she give up on him and find another man of her heart? Where was the one that she met when Eliot was away? Was this the end of the world for Fefe and Eliot? The bitter pain of the lost love gripped her. But she loved Eliot more than she had ever loved anyone.

Even now, she didn't think she could face life without him. But what would she do if the guys had come around and Eliot returned? What would she do if Eliot came back to end their relationship completely? But she felt she was within her rights to feel betrayed and angry, but damn it, he had deliberately fallen in love with Sophie.

He realised that Fefe would never understand his point of view even if he tried to explain why he had chosen to be with Sophie and go with her to France. But there was no point in getting into that right now. It could make things worse than before. Did she care about that? *Things as bad as they could be,* she thought as took her phone again that night. Things were in total jeopardy. She was incandescent with rage.

How dare Eliot choose that woman over me? *she thought angrily.* The nerve of him. She blinked repeatedly. Finally, when the hitmen arrived at her house, she gave them Sophie's address and instructed them to kidnap her. She said that Sophie must be taken to America where she would be used for drug trafficking and other criminal activities. The guys agreed to take the job but knew that they should not rush it. Besides, Sophie had been their long-time victim and quite frankly, Eliot would be one of their victims as well. Right?

Why would Eliot betray her after all the effort she had made? For them? She hovered across the kitchen room and went into the bathroom. She stared at the reflection in the mirror. The pain, hurt, sheer fury and resentment she felt towards him was unspeakable. Why would he keep playing with her feelings for nothing? For another woman? How long had she loved him? Did he really understand what she was going through? Why? Why? Why?

Over and over the question tormented her terribly. Why did he date her in the first place if he didn't want her? If he really didn't love her? What made him change his mind over what they have both agreed to? Had she made him feel pressurised in insisting that they fly together to France or was it just an excuse for him to run away from her? But he knew very well that planning the trip to France and making sure that everything was okay on that day had been a better consideration.

So why must he play her or make her feel hurt because he loved her better than her? She thought angrily. How can he because he was in love with a person whom he just met yesterday? How can he love a person with albinism and choose to undermine her? But now, she never remembered sitting down and thinking about committing herself to one man eternally.

It was only just now that she realised that she made a blunder by being in love with another man before. In fact, it was not a mistake because she had always known that they had been dating and that she had been cheating on Eliot. And now she definitely had to face the consequences. What had she been expecting when she had been cheating on him? Didn't she think that getting sexually transmitted diseases or falling pregnant would be possible?

Clearly, she had taken it for granted that nothing would go wrong. Why get into a relationship otherwise? She thought she was the perfect woman he had wanted her to be. Had she become that particular person he had wanted her to be? She asked herself these questions in dismay. Become the person he wanted her to be rather than be the person she was? What kind of woman would she be if she hadn't become pregnant by another man? Did she consider that?

What kind of a career would she have pursued? Would she have wanted to travel to France if she hadn't dated him? Would she have wanted to fly there for the French Revolution if she hadn't betrayed him? How different would her life have been compared with a person with albinism like Sophie? And why was she sitting there feeling that she sacrificed everything to have that sacrifice flung back in her face when she had already sent the hitmen to kidnap Sophie? Would you say that Fefe really loved Eliot if she sent hitmen to his lover?

On occasion, Eliot had a strange feeling that something terrible was about to happen. He wished he hadn't given Fefe Sophie's residential address. He felt he had made a terrible mistake and that something bad was about to happen to him. He would sit there on the stoep alone and be quiet for a long time, looking far away into space. Most of the days he liked to gaze at the mountains.

When Sophie realised that there was something wrong with him, she asked him what it was but he didn't tell her. He was feeling guilty and frustrated. He had realised the mistake he had made. He shouldn't have gone to see Fefe in the first place. He thought silently and he was still filled with remorse. Every time he had come up with the same answer when asked, "No, I'm fine, don't worry Sophie."

However, this wasn't the truth and he was unwilling to tell her about what he knew. He decided to wait and observe the situation for a while. He made it clear to Fefe that she was not going to accompany him to France.

Despite Eliot denying it, Sophie was concerned that there was something wrong and that he was hiding the truth from her. She needed to know as much as possible but he wasn't ready to do that.

Meanwhile, Fefe wondered what would happen when the hitmen arrived at Sophie's home. She wondered if they would pull the trigger and if Eliot would try to defend his darling. Would he say, "Okay it's fine, take her?" What would Fefe say or do if Eliot was killed? The one thing she knew was that Eliot would defend his lover. She was having second thoughts and wanted the hitmen to abandon their assignment but they were not willing to do so. Even if they decided not to carry out their mission, how would Fefe win back Eliot?

Being frustrated, she hadn't known where she actually stood. Fortunately, when the hitmen arrived at Sophie's place, the couple wasn't around. They had gone out to have some fun. A massive storm was brewing and moving closer. The sounds of the wind and thunder were drowned out by the joyful noise of the family being together, remembering days when Sophie was gone. The hitmen were not concerned about the bad weather.

They parked their car on the pavement and waited. Sophie's sister went outside and saw the car waiting in the street. She wondered who the occupants were. After a while, she went back inside the house and closed the door d closed the door behind her. She made her way to her bedroom without telling her family about the strange car parked on the street. The hitmen grew impatient. They didn't want to waste any more time so they decided to make their presence felt.

As sexy as she had been, Sophie's younger sister who was dressed in a short skirt and a white T-shirt, felt like something horrible was about to happen, and not too long from now. Their double-storey house was old and dilapidated with broken windows in the backroom.

Climbing out of the vehicle, the two hitmen realised that there were a lot of people inside the yard but they weren't who they were looking for. They were looking for Sophie or Eliot. Either one would do for them. Still, Sophie was their main target as Fefe wanted her kidnapped. But what if they found Eliot?

Sophie's sister still had a strange feeling that something bad was about to happen. She tried her best to forget that nagging feeling. The young woman wasn't reading or checking her nails or rather smoking dagga or something. There was something different about that girl. She was simply waiting to fall asleep She couldn't focus on watching television. The thunderstorm was becoming much stronger than when it began earlier that day.

She stood up and walked towards the open window. She always left the window open to allow the cool air in. Standing there with her hands resting on the window, she looked outside and scanned the row of abandoned houses. Nobody wanted to live around here anymore and those other houses were now hollow and dirty. But this young woman in particular had developed a great longing for her home and the rest of her family.

The hitmen could not wait any longer. They stormed the house and their actions were unspeakable. When the young woman saw that the guys were coming inside, she went upstairs and hid in the bathroom. She looked around for a possible escape route but there was no way out except for the one she had just utilised to get access. How long were they going to be in here? Until they had gotten what they were looking for. Until they had eventually found their main priority. But where was Sophie?

"Hey, where is Sophie? Where is Eliot?" one of them asked the family members who were on the front porch. Among them was Linah, Sophie's younger sister who had just come to visit shout but it was late and didn't want to attract unnecessary attention. They cocked their guns in the air. It was a clear warning that if they didn't get what they were looking for, someone would die. Otherwise, someone else would be affected. They were told that the couple was out in town and no one was sure at what time they would be back.

All was silent, including the young woman's breathing. It was getting hot inside the hood. Could oxygen get in here? One family member was hiding under a bed. He forced himself to breathe slowly. If he panicked now, he would be hyperventilate and then...

Sophie's younger sister, Linah, tried to hide behind the bathroom door. She saw the open window and tried to make her way to it. Unfortunately, one of the guys was running upstairs searching for her. While resting her hands on the window frame, she could smell her rank breath and could feel the cold steel of the knife pressing against her back. She refused to relinquish it.

"Hey, you bitch. What do you think you're doing?" the guy asked. She wanted to speak but then paused after being distracted by the noise coming from the living room downstairs. She had definitely known that the guy had company but wasn't sure how many there were. Tactical support. She wanted to scream at him to stay the fuck away but she stayed still, not breaking eye contact but breathing hard.

All the family members were brought into the living room and ordered to lie down next to each other. The other armed guy's expression showed that they were serious and not to be taken lightly. He had pointed a 9mm pistol at them. But the guy upstairs had also wanted to rape Linah. She looked at him for a moment, the fire seemed to die in her eyes. The way he had touched her breasts, it felt as though the guys had come here for something more than what was required of them. He wanted her to pull off her clothes but he couldn't; there was no time for that.

He looked at her for the third time and swallowed hard. He put the knife to her breasts and eventually, he tried to force himself on her but she refused profusely. She had always been a fighter and wondered why people with albinism should be victimised. It was only the two of them upstairs and when she finally refused to be raped by him, he drew out the knife roughly, put it to her throat and cut her trachea. The blood splattered all over the bathroom. The bathroom walls were bloodstained, not to mention the cold tile floor.

When his accomplice realised what he had done, he turned around and took off alone. The family members tried to save Linah's life but It was too late. But who was to blame for all of this? Eliot or Sophie? Now that this terrible thing had happened at Sophie's place, would they still consider going to France?

CHAPTER
Eleven

Her mom, who wanted to die these days, prayed that Sophie would never find out about the death of her younger sister. But there was no reason why she shouldn't find out. In the village, no one knew that Linah had been murdered. Her murderer, Phila, was now behind bars as he never wanted to run off. He had known very well that he would never get away with it, one way or another.

Although he knew that it was wrong that he wanted to rape her, he felt guilty for killing her. he blamed himself for what he had done. He didn't look like a killer, but why kill people with albinism, people who die innocently for nothing? He also felt traitorous anyway for that and almost every mistake he had committed in his whole life.

He knew Eliot very well and wondered what he would say about all this. He wanted to beg him not to be angry with him and that he needed to say that he was sorry that he shouldn't have done this. But he was ready to tell the investigators why he did it and would also confess to reveal the person who had sent them to commit this heinous. But if the woman said no to him, then why did he force himself on her and then eventually kill her?

Fefe wasn't aware of what had transpired. She tried to call the hitmen but none of them answered. They didn't want to talk to her. The one who had fled didn't want to alarm her. He was still on the run. He didn't want to do anything to destroy the opportunity that the police should utilise to arrest her.

He knew she was going to be arrested and go to jail. He also knew that when he turned state witness, he had to be truthful. He wanted to be honest with himself and with everyone and tell the truth as it was. He knew why Fefe had sent them to do the kidnapping and so on. He wondered what she would have done with Sophie if she had been kidnapped. Phila had realised that this was totally wrong, all this madness was wrong.

Why did Fefe want to go with Eliot to France when she clearly knew that he was in love with someone else? Phila thought as he sat in the prison cell, waiting for the pending investigation. He had been worried about Eliot since he committed the crime with his friend two days ago. His phone was confiscated by the police; he knew they had a legal right to do so. He wondered where Eliot was and how stoned he had been. He suspected that Eliot might be arrested for the crime he had committed before but was uncertain if that would really happen.

When they had come back home, Sophie and Eliot were informed about the terrible news. Sophie's tears welled down her cheeks innocently and she wiped them away. She wanted to blame herself and the man she loved for her sister's death. Sitting there on the stool in the kitchen, she just couldn't stop crying. The baby was fast asleep that day.

While the body was at the mortuary Eliot wondered what would happen to him if the police found out he was involved in previous criminal activities. He felt as though he was walking on eggshells for the next three hours. He wasn't tired but made his way to the bedroom out of fear that Sophie's family might confront him and make a scene.

He also feared that they would fight with him and he would be asked to leave the home. When he saw that the walls had been bloodstained in the bathroom, even though it had been half scrubbed, he wept tearfully and silently. He didn't want anyone to know that he was crying. Meanwhile, his lover who had wiped away her remaining tears was in the bedroom and Eliot knew she wanted to be left alone.

He was worried about her but he was glad that he had retreated to the bedroom. He feared if she was still with her family in the living room, she might take it out on him for everything that had happened to them. Inwardly, he blamed himself but he couldn't reveal that to Sophie's family. He just didn't want to deal with the problems now, couldn't avenge anything for he knew that it could make things worse than this. Not today.

He wanted to sit down and be quiet almost the entire day, but it was eight o'clock when he got called in for dinner. His heart was racing. He learnt a lot about this family and everything. He wondered if he and his Sophie would be eventually able to fly to France given what had happened. That night Sophie decided to leave alone and with the baby on her back. When he tried to follow her she furiously refused.

"My younger sister is dead because of you. I just want to be alone please," she cried.

But what did she mean when she said that her sister was dead because of him? She felt as though life or their lives as people with albinism would never be the same again in this world. She felt as though there was no reason for her to live any longer. She never cared, never wanted to get to France anymore and it didn't mean anything to her. But he did. What she knew was that her life was no longer necessary.

The government had been useless and she believed he and his friends in parliament didn't make means to defend the people with albinism. After she had left the baby with her mother, she disappeared. She wanted to die just like her sister. Her mom wondered what she was up to and decided to follow her.

The anger and frustration made her think that she wasn't important anymore or it made her feel as though life itself was stupid. Her mom believed that she would return home and that she just needed some time alone. She wondered why she didn't go away together with Eliot. When she asked Eliot why Sophie was not asked to accompany him to France, he said she had declined the offer. He knew his answer wouldn't go down well. He wondered what really she had been thinking about herself and the baby. The future of their trip to France seemed to have been doomed by the current tragedy.

If he wasn't standing there by the window, he always waited by the gate and lay down there just like a dog, waiting for her to return. After five days, she still had not returned. He was beginning to get more worried than before. Why did he let her go away all on her own? The stupid man! He was full of regret and he still blamed himself for what had happened. He wished he never got involved in the kidnapping game in the first place.

Just thinking about her smile and beauty made him want to go out and look for her. Maybe she was already dead.

Maybe not. He was dismayed. He was utterly crushed. He wondered where he should search to find her. She never came home that night and he was half relieved and half worried when she called him on the phone the following morning. She said that she would be back but didn't say when.

Deep down she knew that she would come back that same day but she wanted him to worry about her and besides, she wanted to see how much he loved her. How much he had bothered himself about her. But life without her at home was a hell of a shit and that was sad too. He remembered what they had once shared and thought of what it could have been like and if they would ever be married.

He wondered if they ever had or if the relationship had been doomed from the beginning. But he hadn't wanted to believe that then. He still remembered their honeymoon in Cape Town and how sweet he had been to her at the time. But, it wasn't enough anymore. It didn't compensate for the agony he and his friends had caused her family members, worrying about them day and night. He couldn't afford to think about that now, neither the good times nor the bad. He had to concentrate on finding out if she was still alive.

That was all he could think of now. Even now, he still loved her and wanted nothing but the best for her. He still longed a lot for their trip to France, regardless of the situation. As confused, angry and hurt as she was, he believed that there was no love lost between them and that their romance would turn them into Romeo and Juliet, escaping the Montagues and Capulets which in this case, would be their hitmen. He wanted to explain how much he was dying inside him for her, but did he have to do that? Was she going to be interested in that matter and what was he expecting her to do after that?

He had been thinking hard and he took a breath slowly. Even after the funeral, the woman he loved so much acted as if she wasn't interested in him and she wasn't sure what was going on with her and how long that bitter feeling would last. Sophie couldn't just forget what had happened to her younger sister. Every time she looked at her photos on the walls and in the album, she cried uncontrollably.

But who was to blame for her murder? Was she certain that her husband had nothing to do with it? Besides, she and Eliot were together and away from home when this ruthless incident happened. So why should she blame him? Every time she looked at him in the face she wanted to tell him that she had lost her blood sister, she had lost a lot all because of him. But she couldn't. Maybe she was waiting for the right time to do that.

Besides, there was something else she realised about politics and that ever since Dr Nelson Mandela had died everything was uncontrollable in the country. That everyone did things according to their wishes. That people can just kidnap others and kill them as though they were nothing. But the government now seems not to be fair and all the government officials are focusing on how they benefit financially. She blamed the government as a whole too, that they hardly consider the people first.

She was of the strong belief that in South Africa, people were never put first. Where are they going to end up if the people with albinism continue to be slaughtered for rituals and financial benefits? He figured he was going to talk to Sophie once she had calmed down. But when exactly? What if he was too late by the time he approached her? Her mother had once told her that she should not treat him how she wanted. She understood the way she had been feeling but her hatred and stubbornness was not going to help the situation.

"But Mama, I feel like I can't do it anymore, you see?" Sophie explained briefly to her mom as they chatted in the garden in the backyard. The birds were singing harmoniously and it reminded her of the day they visited the lake.

"But he is the father of your children." The mother had been so defensive and seemed to guarantee this matter. "No, Mom. Just look at what happened to my younger sister. Just imagine the way she brutally lost her life."
"But who did it then?"
"Whose friends were they by the way?"

"I want to tell you something, my dear."

"What is it Mother?" Her mom took a little while before she explained it to her. She wanted Sophie to understand it very well, regardless of her anger and frustration. She knew how sad she was following the death of her younger sister but the was nothing they could do to undo it.

"Would you kindly stand by him? Please dear. Besides, if you dump him how many men are you going to continue to dump?" Sophie could not answer. Instead, she turned to look and the mountains and the rivers in the distance. Then, her mom asked her one last question, "Are you still going to fly together for the French Revolution?"

Sophie turned around to look at her mom and shook her head. She implied that it was no longer in her heart and that she wasn't promising anything. Not now. Not after the death of her younger sister. Her mother had begged her so much that she mustn't just make him feel hurt for what he didn't do. She told her how Eliot had been so kind and calm to both her and the rest of the family. She even emphasised that he had never abused her either physically or mentally.

What she knew was that her mom would never force her to continue to be in love with him. Sophie was supposed to learn more about life. That the life of today is very crucial but ruthless at the same time. That no man could be kind and ruthless at the same time. Who can say it? But they both knew that it could be more than that and before sunset, Sophie tried to soften him. What if tonight was the last time they were together?

She couldn't answer that question, They were in the bedroom when they leaned towards each other and she kissed him wildly. She wondered if they would ever kiss like that again. It was a gentle kiss at first, but it was rapidly warmed by the passion she felt and the fact that he took her in her arms and held her tight. His grip was strong and his lips pressed hard against hers. After she pulled away, she was breathless. She said nothing but the look in her eyes said it all. Suddenly, as he kissed her, he got up from the bed with a look of regret. She didn't want or expect him to remind her about the visit to France. She knew that he could. Lying there on the side of the bed, he smiled at her with a tender look that warmed her heart.

"Can you please try not to disappoint us on the French Revolution matter? It's still very important to us my darling," he said it. She turned to look at him and he kissed her again and this time the heart of passion was his as she seemed to melt in his arms. He could feel the satin of her dress come away from her flesh beneath his fingers. She stood in front of him and that's when they heard the baby crying in the dining room. She assumed he was hungry because he hadn't eaten anything since the afternoon. She wondered if she should still go to France

and have some while she was still grieving the death of
her sister.

139

CHAPTER
Twelve

On the day before the police showed up at Sophie's home, Eliot was in pretty good shape. The police didn't let anyone know about their impending visit. That day it looked as though it was the last time when he would utter those romantic words to the only woman he truly loved. "You look so beautiful *maan*," he said with a wide smile.

"Thank you very much," she responded with a gorgeous smile. It was such a sweet smile, one he would never forget in his entire life. She was in the living room drinking a tasteful wine that Eliot had bought earlier in the day. It was such a magical day and Sophie drank more than she normally would have done.

On that day she was so comfortable with him and even though things had been difficult for her, it seemed perfectly natural when he leaned over and kissed her softly on the lips. However, he did nothing more than that. He wanted to smile again but instead, he kissed her again, and she felt her entire body long for his touch. Then she suddenly moved closer to him and gently touched his chest, and she wasn't sure what to say. She felt totally at ease and she wished that he could have been here long before he had come to live here with her. More than a hundred years of course.

Many other girls seemed to be coming in and out, but she didn't worry about them. She hadn't slept with him for several months now and she was suddenly desperately hungry for him. She sat beside him. How proud and happy he must have felt, just like a king, you know. Lately, she had been grateful to be with him. She didn't want to be alone, especially in the bedroom.

The upstairs area did not look good and smelled of beer but most people inside all looked young, healthy and clean. He realised that most of them were people with albinism. But on the days when she was away, she had been feeling both exhilarated and depressed at the same time. Depressed about what had happened to her younger sister but she hoped that it would pass bit by bit as time went on.. Depressed about the way things were between herself and her boyfriend. At the same time, she felt exhilarated to be with him. She was always feeling at ease when she was with him.

Lately, there was something very special about their relationship. But they both didn't understand what it was. The way she felt for him, it was as though she was replacing someone who had just died. She looked at him and kissed him and held him close for a long time and when he looked at her again, it was already dark outside. The funny thing was that he needed her too, more than he knew what to say; more than what he wanted to admit.

They lay on the bed until she fell asleep, exhausted by the emotions of the day. It was just after he had switched off the lights in the bedroom, so he lay in the dark, looking at her, holding her close. But he didn't do anything. He just lay there next to her, crying when he thought about the past and how desperately he wanted her.

Eliot heard the whining vehicles outside on the street. He didn't understand what had been happening out there or who it was. Initially, he wanted to go downstairs and make some coffee for himself. But his instincts were telling him that something terrible was about to happen to him. He looked around the bedroom and at the same time wanted to ignore the abnormal noise and pollution in the atmosphere. He stood up and went downstairs but he didn't make it as anticipated. He suddenly developed cravings for tea.

He decided to go back upstairs and looked out of the landing window. The noise on the street went on and one couldn't stop it. His breath caught up in his throat as he saw the cars waiting still in the streets. He grew faint. He inhaled deeply and stood at the top of the stairs waiting for anything that could happen. But then he still seemed to ignore the matter as it was. He was both amazed and frustrated by the quietness that engulfed the entire world. Although it was so quiet, he knew that he should have read the book, *I Will Marry When I Want* by Ngugi Wathiongo but he couldn't.

"Damn it!" he said. He didn't sound happy about the presence of the vehicles outside. He couldn't identify who the people were exactly and why they had come here. He looked like a frightened broken child. But he knew that he shouldn't go down there or else... He stood alone in that position, the innocent tears falling down his cheeks. He was terrified and felt like he would never see his lover again. If someone entered the house and took him away, he would have whispered these painful words to her, "Goodbye my love. I will always love you." He was not willing to go anywhere but he was certain that something bad was about to happen to him. He still wanted to go with her but he wasn't going to force her and she wasn't sure if they would fly together.

Will the trip to France still be possible under these cruel circumstances? he thought nervously. He didn't have an answer to that question. He also wondered what Sophie had thought about when she had left the house a few days ago. But honestly, she would have not been with another man. Then the police officer went to knock at the door. There were four police cars parked in the street. Their lights were flashing. Eliot had a terrible sense of impending doom. He hurried breathlessly down the narrow passage and opened the door.

The downstairs part of the house was cold and it was windy outside. The policemen looked calm but serious. More officers were waiting outside the house. After a few minutes of brief interrogation, the police went away. Eliot had a good alibi as the night that Linah was murdered, he and Sophie were out having fun somewhere else. As a result, he escaped being arrested. He should have been in jail by now. But prison life wasn't part of him or where he belonged either. Sometimes, he felt devastated when he thought that they might return to try to arrest him again.

Did he feel guilty that the police approached him for the death of the young albino woman? But what would happen to him if they came back to him again? What would he do when they come in for\him? What if they had already suspected him to be one of the conspirators or murderers? What was he feeling now?

However, he felt warmed by Sophie's loyalty. He knew that the death of the woman was extremely tragic but he wanted the entire family to forgive and forget that it had happened. On the other hand, he despised and condemned the assassins for all the hurt and pain they had caused to Sophie's family. He hoped that his friends and other family members would support the ones who were feeling hurt at the moment. *The assassins will be sorry,* he thought viciously. He wondered what would happen to him if things went sour between himself and the woman he loved.

Nothing was worrying him like the police visits and the escalating investigations. He still loved her more than he had ever loved anyone in this world. He couldn't face life without her. What would he do if she decided to leave him for good this time? After several police visits, Sophie advised him to leave for another place where he would be safe. That was the only way the police would stop bothering him. That didn't mean she didn't love him anymore. But he felt the other way round, as though she didn't want him anymore. And that maybe she was in love with someone else. But that was the total opposite of what he was thinking. Still, he was pissed off at her suggestion.

"Just go away, and that way you will survive," she said and she cried. Her tears were all for him. But she knew that he wasn't ready to leave. He was only concerned about the journey to France.

"But I can't live without you, and you know that, Don't you?" he replied defensively. He wanted to weep uncontrollably. By the way he looked at her, one would think that he had bad intentions against her.

Packing up the bags, he stood still at the door trying to calm the turmoil raging within him. But he felt it was not his fault that Linah had been murdered. And yet he was feeling guilty for what he didn't do. Had he taken far too much for granted and not put in enough effort pandering to her and her needs? But what about the way he had been feeling for her?

But the previous time he hadn't pandered to her in any way out of the ordinary love, he thought resentfully. And that he wasn't part and parcel of what it was all about. No couple could spend their entire time navel-gazing their relationship, he again thought irritably. He hadn't eaten the whole day. Maybe he should ignore it. He wasn't going to eat while he felt as though he was being dumped far away for nothing. Or wasn't he? He still loved her with his whole heart.

How was he going to survive without her by his side? Why would she want him to leave under these terrible night-mares? Why would she force him to go away when he didn't want to? Didn't he realise that she was protecting him? "But I can't go away without you. You see?" he said as he swallowed hard. "But you will be arrested and go to jail after that. Can't you see that Eliot?" she replied. He felt like she was trying to avoid him or something by wanting him to leave. He really couldn't understand why she wanted him to leave. What was he going to do now? Did he really have to go away without her next to him? It was a blustery day of dark tranches of clouds interspersed with light. It felt very strange to be waiting there aimlessly and he wondered if he should go. Where was he supposed to go to? Should he do that? Or should he go straight to Sophie's mother and tell her that he had no intention of leaving the house?

She wanted him to protect her but there was nothing Sophie's mother could do if her daughter was pushing him to go. But if he had gone away alone, he wondered if they would ever be together again. Was this the end or the start of his whole new life? What about her and their three children who would have to live without him? He thought with a trembling hand. But he knew that he shouldn't protest anyway.

Wasn't this what he wanted for so long? Freedom. Well, he was given it now. And somehow, having it wasn't the same as wanting it. It would be better if she played it cool and kept him on his toes. Besides, the worst thing in the world for him was to be smothered by her. The encounter with Sophie had shaken him. Pushing him away that way after more than fifteen years must have been very difficult for him psychologically, no matter how she felt or how right she was about the decision to ask him to leave.

He felt as though there would be rocky times ahead of him and he would have to weather them and was not sure if he could. He decided not to leave. What would she do then? Didn't she understand that he loved her no matter what? *Does she know the meaning of love, the pain of love and the feeling of being rejected by someone you really love?* he thought, wanting to defend himself again.

Short of physically throwing him out or making him go, she couldn't force him to go. It could end up in a situation where she would want to move out herself. But she didn't know whether to feel sorry or glad about his decision. But why was he concerned about the flight to France and why was it so important to him? According to him, it would be better if he got arrested only after the visit to France.

If he had managed to get there with or without her, then he knew that his dream would have been fulfilled. Wasn't that good enough for him? Even on the seventh night she went to hold him tightly, kissed him softly but she couldn't leave his arms. Was that the final time she would kiss him that way?

He wondered what the reason behind her behaviour was—the meaning behind the way she touched him. He couldn't forget the taste of her sweet mouth. That this was the only thing that had ever made him feel like a king or more than that. It made him feel as though he had finally won the trip to France and that he would be highly recognised worldwide for the fact he would be having a good conversation with the French government about the French Revolution.

He realised that lately, their romance had been alive and blazing. But the main thing was that he had the feeling that he had won her whole heart at last. But then he had never known that four days later he would be disappointed that Sophie had gone missing. He didn't know what had happened to her or how it had taken place.

When he woke up in the morning he found that she wasn't there next to him in bed. The bedroom felt cold. It felt so ridiculous as though he had been fooled. *But why has she disappeared once again?* he thought grimly. He stood by the bedroom door and exhaled deeply. He turned around and went to lean backwards by the bedroom window, his hands resting on the window frame. This was what he normally did when he had an emotional problem such as this one.

Thinking about her, his chest felt so tight with grief that he could hardly breathe. But then he felt belittled, fooled and worthless. How would he ever get through this? Was this the way he was going to feel for the rest of his life? For the first time, he could understand why many people committed suicide. His future seemed empty and dark, full of despair and humiliation. His struggle was more than he had anticipated.

He remembered the first time he and Sophie had met, the beautiful days together of course. He missed the feeling of the touch of her soft hands and looking into her beautiful eyes. The beautiful smile and the gorgeous looks, all that was something he would never forget. He had discovered something very special about women with albinism: the amazing touch and the kiss that had been beyond him.

CHAPTER
Thirteen

A few days later the police return. Eliot seemed to have been bothered by their visits and their routine of endless questioning. He waited at the door downstairs as though he was the house owner, folding his strong arms across his chest.

"Are you Eliot Maphasa?" one of the officers asked as if he was about to arrest him. He took a minute before he could answer that question. But he wondered why his name was required by them.

"Yes, of course I am. Why?" He wanted to know the reason why they were asking for his name. It sounded very serious. He began to panic.

"What do you know about the death of the woman, Sophie?" the officer asked. He started trembling as though he knew what had already happened to his lover whom he should have married a long time ago.

"What? The death....?" He didn't want to believe what the police had just said to him. What did they mean when the officer said, "The death of the woman, Sophie?" He wondered what had happened to his lover. "Yes, when last have you last seen her?"

"Four days ago."
"Did you fight with her before she disappeared?"
"No, why would I?"
"Is there anyone here on the farm who might want to kill her?"
"I'm not really sure about that."

"She was found dead in a shack in the dark forest in a shack. She had been brutally murdered."

Eliot bent his head slightly and wept tearfully but loudly. Prison life seemed to be possible now. She died right where she was once kept hostage by him all those years ago when he was still a monster, a criminal.

"Do you know that forest?" the detective asked as he looked directly into Eliot's eyes. "What forest are you talking about now?" He pretended not to know it but he clearly remembered it very well. He reacted angrily when he was asked about the dark forest. But actually, he understood that matter.

The investigators turned to look at each other and one of them smiled slyly as they realised that he was trying to hide something. Why ask questions about what had happened a long time ago? Eliot was very worried. There was a silence that lasted longer than it should have. The ivestigators didn't rush things as they spoke to him and the other three didn't respond but dug deep into their pockets.

Was this the end of his life? Wasn't that the end of the future French Revolution and the trip for him? He almost fell into a deep sleep but woke up two hours in. It was late in the afternoon when he made his way downstairs and stood by the doorway.

He had always hoped that he would see her again and then their lives would go on again. But when he got into the world of kidnapping and crime, what had he thought through his mind? Didn't he think that one day the wheel would turn on him? He thought he would end up losing an appetite when he assumed that the police might come up with something else again, asking him about this and that.

He hated being questioned by them all the time when he was still depressed about his darling. He felt he would always love her, felt he would always miss her and the comfortable touch of love within her heart. He would never feel that way with another woman. Still, he wanted the police to stop showing up and asking him questions about a matter he was not involved in.

Why would he kill someone that he truly loved? Why must he kill the woman who had taught him things that he had never anticipated when he adored her with his whole heart? Even though he had lost her eternally, he would never forget his children. Nor would he forget her. All of his biological kids had always made him think about Sophie's smile. She had gone too soon but would never be forgotten.

In the evening he went to the bedroom upstairs, switched on the lamp, drew the curtains and eventually sat on the edge of the bed and thought again. He comfortably covered his head in his hands as he bent down. He wondered what would happen to him if the police came back and arrested him. What would happen to his only children if he was convicted and sent to prison? He desperately prayed that their granny wouldn't die so that she could look after them and protect them. But he couldn't predict what his ultimate fate would be.

However, he hoped that God would protect them as long as he was alive and still around his family. What he wanted from God was the last pity. But he didn't want to test His total integrity. *Or otherwise...,* he thought with a stupid smile. He was still downstairs when it began to rain. There was nowhere he could flee and he felt guilty as though he had killed his lover. He wished they could have got married. But it was too late now. If it was possible to do so posthumously perhaps it would have been fine with him.

He missed her entire being, her soft touch and of course, the last kiss they shared. He wondered if another woman would kiss him the way she did. He wondered how she possibly knew how to kiss him like that. She was the one who had made him become the person he is today, the father of their children. This was the permanent title he would never forget through his whole life. *Why am I so bloody unfortunate?* he thought sorrowfully as he stood up and walked to the door. It was still open when the police turned up again.

It was dusk when they knocked hard on the door. He knew something bad was about to happen. He sighed deeply as he put his arms across his chest. *What is it now?* he thought. He felt utterly crushed. He was terribly unsettled when he was questioned again. He felt as though his future for the French Revolution would be over, but he had to get on with it. And he knew it. But it was frustrating and when he saw Fefe behind the white police van, he almost fainted. He could see that it had been a great upheaval in his life but it was time that he faced facts.

Why can't he get on with enjoying life with himself? Why didn't he forget about Sophie and the French Revolution and so on? But it could be so much good if only he would relax and let go of the past. He knew and had a guarantee that Fefe must have sold him out together with the hitmen. He didn't know that the other hitman who ran away on the night after Linah was murdered got arrested too. He was obviously in trouble as he saw his accomplice being handcuffed in the front seat of the police car.

There were more than seven police vehicles parked on the sidewalk and they remained there for some time. But the farm had been so much older than the previous years, and he missed those lovely days being with his late darling. But he wondered if those beautiful days would ever come back again. What he knew was that he would never love another woman like his albino lover.

But why were men attracted to women with albinism? What did they give these men that other black women didn't give to them to make them always feel happy and satisfied? He thought about this as he was told to get into the van, the same van where Fefe was sitting. She seemed to have betrayed him at last. Her betrayal made him angry and he refused to look at her.

Why would the police officers make him share the same van with this bloody woman? Why should they keep testing his integrity when he wasn't even happy about the death of his late lover? What kind of police officers were they? What kind of life was this and can he undo all this mess? Must he forget about the French Revolution? But who was Fefe for him to take a flight with her abroad? And why?

His thoughts were running fast and he couldn't stop them. He had learnt a lesson from her but can he forget what she had done to him? Can she understand how he was betrayed by her own guard?